MARRYING
HIS RUNAWAY
HEIRESS

MARRYING HIS RUNAWAY HEIRESS

THERESE BEHARRIE

MILLS & BOON

First published in Great Britain 2020
by Mills & Boon, an imprint of HarperCollins*Publishers*
1 London Bridge Street, London, SE1 9GF

Large Print edition 2020

© 2020 Therese Beharrie

ISBN: 978-0-263-08508-2

MIX
Paper from
responsible sources
FSC˚ C007454

This book is produced from independently certified FSC™ paper to ensure responsible forest management. For more information visit www.harpercollins.co.uk/green.

Printed and bound in Great Britain
by CPI Group (UK) Ltd, Croydon, CR0 4YY

For Grant, because he's the reason
I experienced Italy and its beauty and
romance. I think—by law—that means
I have to dedicate this book to him.

Also because he loves me
unconditionally, which never fails
to surprise and overwhelm me.
Thank you.

CHAPTER ONE

IF ELENA JOHN hadn't known better, she'd have thought Micah Williams was simply being thoughtful. But she did know better. He wasn't being thoughtful; he was trying to charm her. Soften her up.

If they'd met before she would have told him not to bother.

Instead, she climbed into the limousine that had pulled up in front of her house with a resigned sigh. It was as luxurious on the inside as it was on the outside. In one corner a minibar packed with her favourite drinks—which couldn't be a coincidence since her favourite drinks were undeniably strange—and a basket of snacks in another corner. Music streamed through the speakers. Soft, unassuming, bland music no one could find offensive. Then there was the driver, who checked on her constantly, and the flight attendant, who took over from the driver once Elena reached the airport.

The longer she thought about it though, the more she liked the idea of Mr Williams trying to charm her. It wouldn't work, but the fact that he was trying reminded her of what she'd accomplished. Five years at her newspaper and finally, *finally* she'd got assigned an important story. A story about a powerful man. Now, the powerful man was trying to nudge her towards writing a good story. She'd shadowed enough journalists, transcribed enough interviews, heard enough stories to know sometimes people did that.

She'd spent enough time with powerful men to know sometimes they did that, too.

Considering the situation she was leaving behind, the thought that Mr Williams was trying to manipulate her should have angered her. But this was for her job. She had prepared for this her entire career. And for once, she wasn't the one in the helpless position. So what if the limousines and private planes, the obedient and careful staff, and the access to her favourite things reminded her of the first sixteen years of her life?

It might be a precursor to the next years of your life, too.

The thought made her faintly nauseous.

'Ms John?' The flight attendant was staring at her, his spine so straight, his posture so poised, she wanted to know if he'd practised it. 'Through here.'

'Yes.'

She followed him through the blue velvet curtain into the plush luxury of Micah Williams's private plane. The design was different from her father's, which was mostly for efficiency and productivity. Here the open space was a balance of that and relaxation, with comfortable-looking chairs on either side of the aisle in front of a modern desk. The biggest difference though was the man standing in front of that desk.

Micah Williams.

He was handsome. She didn't bother tiptoeing around it. His skin was an awe-inspiring shade of brown, as if the heavens had opened and a stream of both light and dark shone on him. His body was clad in a suit that was made for his broad shoulders, his narrow waist, his long legs. His hair was dark and short, his stubble a length that told her it had been purposefully groomed that way. None of it was a surprise. Her research had prepared her.

What surprised her was the intensity of his gaze. The way he looked at her as if she had the answer to a question he'd had all his life. She wasn't prepared for how his mouth curved at the side when he realised she was staring. When she realised he was staring right back.

She resisted the urge to smooth down the red pants suit she wore. She still wore her black coat over it, but the red was visible. She'd purposefully chosen to wear the colour. It was *her* colour. That knowledge was one of the few things her mother had left her before she'd packed her bags to travel the world.

Having a colour made Elena feel good; being in her colour made her feel strong. Strength helped her accept that this man was staring at her so intensely.

'Ms John,' he said smoothly, stepping forward. 'Thank you for coming.'

'Did I have a choice?' she asked lightly. She gave herself a moment to enjoy his surprise. It flitted over the intensity, making it seem lighter. She knew it was an illusion. 'It's a free trip to Italy.'

Something twitched on his face. 'That's what you meant, is it?' His tone was dry. 'It has nothing to do with this being for your job?'

'No. It's all about a gondola ride.'

'You've been on a gondola before,' he said confidently.

'No.' She searched his face. 'Why does that surprise you?'

'For the same reason I don't believe you need a free trip to Italy.'

He knew who she was.

She schooled her face, trying hard not to give in to disappointment. It wasn't the end of the world. Her identity wasn't a secret. But— did this mean what she thought it meant? The only way to find out was to ask.

'Are you referring to the fact that my family owns the John Diamond Company?'

The intense look was back. Bemusement was there, too.

'I am.'

'Is that why I'm here, Mr Williams? Because of my family?'

The seconds ticked by. Eventually, he said, 'It is.'

She sighed. 'Wonderful.' Paused. 'Your attempts to butter me up were ridiculous, by the way.' It was an immature comment, and nowhere near an appropriate response to what he was admitting or the implications of it. But he didn't get a chance to answer her.

'We're about to take off,' the flight attendant said behind her. 'Can you please take your seats?'

She settled in a seat next to the window. Tried to steady herself by looking out at the city she loved. There was nothing on the tarmac besides a few other planes. Bright green grass was scattered beyond the tar, the dew of the brisk day settling on it. If she looked close enough, she'd swear she'd find ice sitting on the tips of the blades of grass. If nothing else, she was leaving a cold, wet South Africa for a sunny, warm Italy. If nothing else, she was leaving behind two men who thought they could control her life.

You're thinking about letting them though.

She exhaled slowly.

'I've upset you.'

They were in the air already, though barely, when Micah spoke.

'No.' She kept her gaze on the window. Outside it was all blue now, with white puffs of clouds around them. 'Why would you think that?'

'You insulted my attempts at cordiality.'

She almost laughed at the indignation in his voice. 'So try harder next time.'

A strangled sound came from the vicinity of his seat. She allowed herself to enjoy it, but didn't turn to look at him, or let him see her smile. It was a while longer before he said anything again.

'I didn't only ask for you to do this story because of your name, you know.'

So he had asked for her. Which meant that she likely hadn't earned this assignment as she initially believed. And she was more helpless than she initially believed. It smarted, and the sting of it coated her tongue, slipping into her words, her tone.

'I'm sure. It's those pop culture articles I wrote, isn't it? Speculating on who someone will end up with next truly does display the depth of my talent.'

'I did enjoy the article about the ex-rugby player bad boy who faked a relationship but fell in love for real.'

At that, Elena turned to look at him. He was sitting on the only other seat opposite her, lounging back in his chair, watching her as if he had nothing else to do. Elena knew that couldn't be true. The man ran an empire. His business had grown immensely in the ten years since he'd started it. His company sold luxury goods in Africa, primarily South Africa, and he'd recently partnered with two non-African brands worth millions to do that for. She suspected another brand would be added to that in Italy.

It was all part of why Elena's newspaper had selected him as their Businessperson of the Year. She was supposed to be writing an article about how amazingly busy he was. There was no way he had time to converse with her.

'You read that?'

'I did.'

He flicked a forearm out, rolled back his shirt sleeve. He did the same on the other side. She watched, stuck on the fact that he'd taken off his suit jacket. Also, on his forearms. His *forearms*. They were muscular, with lines of veins that looked as if they were pulsing. They made her want to trace them with her fingertips, then grip that swelling just before his elbow to feel the muscle there. She wanted to—

Nothing. She wanted to nothing.

What did Jameson's forearms look like? Did it matter? The marriage he and her father had proposed was purely business. Purely name. Which made what Micah had done sting sharper. She was there for her name, too. Not for his admittedly good-looking forearms.

Wait—Micah? When had she started calling him Micah?

'I have to admit, there was a lot of speculation, even in that.'

Okay, he was speaking again. Yes, right. She needed to reply. That was how conversations worked. If she remembered correctly, and honestly, she wasn't sure she did.

'Pop culture articles are speculative by nature. Unless you have a reliable source, but that changes things. The tone of the article. It shifts the attention. You have people focusing more on who the source could be as opposed to the content. Generally, I use sources for articles that are already more fact than opinion. Which, I guess, is the difference between having my piece in the entertainment section of the printed paper versus only the digital edition.'

The silence that followed her answer alerted her to how much she'd said. She'd surprised them both with it, but she refused to feel embarrassed. She knew what she was doing. Writing was not only her job, but her passion. She read articles and books on writing, did online courses, followed noted journalists on social media. All of this was over and above her responsibilities at the newspaper.

She was *capable.* It was part of why Micah Williams asking for her annoyed her. He shouldn't have had to ask; she should have been given this. She deserved it.

'This is exactly why I thought you'd do well on this article,' Micah said. 'There was something about your work that felt intentional. Even the fluff pieces, which I enjoyed immensely.'

'How could you not?' she countered. 'Everyone knows how much people enjoy fluff.'

He laughed. It was surprising and arousing. At that point, Elena should have known she was already in trouble. Then he said, 'Ms

John, you'll quickly discover that my tastes aren't similar to most people's.' There was a slight pause. 'I'm going to enjoy showing you that.'

The fact that she *wanted* him to show her? That she thought she would *enjoy* it? Oh, yeah. Trouble.

Micah Williams hadn't expected the John heiress to be so…

Interesting.

The word seemed woefully inadequate to describe the woman sitting opposite him. As a result, he watched her more than was necessary. Her expressions were animated, her tone dry and sharp in equal measure, and she was surprisingly candid. Surprisingly attractive, too.

Not her appearance. He'd seen that in pictures. The wild, curly hair. The gloss of her brown skin and the dusting of freckles on only her left cheek, though that detail hadn't been clear in the pictures. He noted it now because it had a certain charm. As did the way her mouth was painted bright red. Her lips were full, plump, and he'd experienced plenty of people in his lifetime who would have been embarrassed by that abundance. Ms John seemed to have embraced it.

That peek into her personality was really the most attractive thing about her.

She embraced plenty of things, it seemed. The admittedly extra nature of how he'd brought her to his plane—not that he'd expected her to point it out. The fact that he knew who she was. That he'd requested her for the article. Micah hadn't expected it to be easy to get Elena on his side, but now he thought her honesty might aid him. Maybe that was why he offered her such honesty in return.

Either that, or those red lips. And that luscious body, tall and curved, clad in a red pants suit visible despite her coat. The white T-shirt she wore beneath it clung to ample breasts. And her heels, white as well, highlighted the most beautiful set of ankles he'd seen in his life.

He blinked. Ankles? Since when had he noticed a woman's ankles? Of all the things he'd been attracted to, ankles had never appeared on the list. His eyes lowered to her legs. She'd crossed them.

So maybe he simply hadn't seen the *right* pair of ankles.

Interesting. Irrelevant, but interesting.

'Do you know, if you'd started our conversation with the fact that you've read my work, things would have been a lot less contentious?'

'Contentious?' he repeated. 'I don't know what you mean, Ms John.'

'Elena, please.' There was a slight pause. She hesitated. Undid her seat belt and stood, offering him a hand. 'I'm sorry. I didn't introduce myself properly. I am Elena.'

She didn't say her surname. He stored it into the vault of information he had about her, undid his own seat belt, and stood.

'Micah.'

'Good to meet you, Mr Williams.'

She took his hand. Shook in two quick pumps. It shouldn't have heated his blood. Shouldn't have had any effect on him whatsoever.

It did.

'If I call you Elena, you'll have to call me Micah,' he said, hoping to heaven his voice was normal and not tinted with the desire he suddenly felt.

'It feels…' she hesitated '…wrong to call you Micah.'

'Wrong?' Another interesting fact. 'How so?'

'Unprofessional,' she clarified.

'This is about the article.'

'Yes, of course.' She frowned. 'What else could it be about?'

This unexpected attraction between us?

'Nothing else. We're on the same page.'

He pressed the button that called the flight attendant, and when the man appeared ordered himself a drink. With alcohol. To shock his system into behaving. Elena ordered a water. There was that professionalism again. It obviously meant a lot to her. But why?

'I promise not to consider you unprofessional if you use my first name,' he said, accepting the glass from the flight attendant. 'I won't tell anyone at the newspaper either.'

'Thank you.' Her tone was somehow a mixture of dryness and gratitude. Fascinating creature, the John heiress. 'I'll call you Micah—' he ignored the thrill that beat in his heart '—for the duration of this week. Since we are spending it together, it might be strange to continue speaking to you so formally.' She didn't give him a chance to process before she was asking, 'Is the itinerary for this week finalised?'

She was putting distance between them, he realised. He kept his smile to himself. He wasn't sure what was amusing him more: the fact that she felt the need to put distance between them when they'd barely known one another for an hour; or how seamlessly she'd done so. He was being managed. Expertly. He hadn't thought much about how her being an heiress would affect this business trip. Well, other than his plan to endear himself to her. But now he was experiencing it.

A journalist had never put him in his place so skilfully before. Nor a woman. He barely felt that he'd been moved, let alone gently, if firmly, lowered to the ground. It was tied into the professionalism somehow. The attraction. He had no idea—and he wanted to know. Except that wasn't why she was here. He needed to remember that.

'It is. The one my assistant emailed to you is accurate, apart from two meetings that I have scheduled for our last day in Rome. It was the only time my client was available,' he added apologetically.

'You don't have to explain,' she said with a shake of her head. 'I know how it goes with business trips.'

'I imagine you do.'

Her brow lifted, but she didn't engage. 'Is there a reason Serena isn't joining us?'

'I wanted time to speak with you.'

'That's why you don't have your laptop open either?'

'I wouldn't have my laptop open when I have a guest.'

She laughed. It was a light, bubbly sound he found delightful. Again, not relevant.

'We both know guests don't get in the way of business, Micah.'

He lifted his glass to his lips thoughtfully. 'I'm beginning to think your experience of business and the way I conduct mine are different.'

She studied him for a moment, then reached into the huge white handbag she'd brought with her and pulled out her phone. She pressed a few buttons, and suddenly a large red dot was gleaming up at him.

'I'm beginning to think so, too,' she replied, despite the minutes that had passed. 'Why don't we start talking about those differences?' She touched her finger to her phone's screen. The device began recording. 'What inspired you to start this business, Mr Williams?'

An expert at managing, he thought again, and answered her.

CHAPTER TWO

Micah Williams was too suave for his own good. Or for Elena's own good. She wanted to get beneath the businessperson persona. That wasn't part of her job, obviously. She was only meant to portray the businessperson. She had enough of the basics to write a good introduction. She could already see it.

Micah Williams is charming, but ruthless—a fact he wouldn't want you to believe. The latter, that is. He enjoys his charm almost as much as he thinks his audience does. And perhaps his audience does.

His eyes light up when he talks business, though there's always an intensity shadowed there, regardless of the business topic. He knows just what to say and he relishes saying it, knowing it's exactly what he should be saying.

But it's in that very fact that his ruthlessness lies. Williams has no qualms about telling you what you want to hear even as he uses what you don't want to hear against you. He's a lion, circling his prey, if the lion was tall and handsome, and—

Maybe she needed to work on that last line.

But the sentiment remained. Micah was giving her information she could have surmised from the handful of interviews he'd done before her.

She was good at reading people through what they didn't say as much as through what they did. It was what made her so good at writing pop culture pieces. She could deduce what people wanted the public to know and what they didn't. So she narrowed in on what they didn't; there was almost always a story there.

There was definitely more to Micah's success than 'hard work and good luck'. It had something to do with both his charm and his ruthlessness. If he so much as got a whiff of the fact that she thought him ruthless though, he'd protest. He was trying much too hard to get her to believe he was a harmless domestic animal.

He was definitely a lion. Nothing else.

She particularly knew it because of the way he was circling around her family.

She refused to indulge him.

'Can we take a break?' he asked after they'd been talking for an hour. 'I'm starving.'

Since they'd covered a lot more than she thought they would on the first day, travelling, she said, 'Sure. Will we be eating Chef Gardner or Ike today?'

He smiled. 'You've done your research.'

'I'm insulted you thought otherwise.'

'Wouldn't want that,' he purred. 'I apologise.'

She stared. 'You aren't as charming as you think you are, you know.'

His eyelashes fluttered. She mentally patted herself on the back for surprising him.

'I have no idea what I did to deserve that.'

'Of course you don't. You're on, all the time. It means you don't have time to reflect. Probably,' she added in the unlikely event that she was wrong.

His jaw tightened. 'Presumptuous.'

He wasn't trying to hide that he didn't like that comment. It was the first authentic reaction she'd seen from him—the first one that wasn't an acceptable reaction—and it made her heart thud.

'Journalists presume until they don't have to,' she said.

'Journalists?' There was a deliberate pause. 'Or heiresses?'

When threatened, a lion would attack. Micah had done just that to the elephant in the room.

An uncomfortable ripple went through her, but she was saved from replying when the flight attendant came in and took their orders for food. She was going to be eating steak on a plane, which was the kind of food she'd forgotten about eating on a plane since her parents had divorced. Her life had changed then.

If only it had changed enough for her to stop trying to please her unpleasable father.

'You're offended,' he commented after the flight attendant left. His expression was smooth again, as if he hadn't shown he was human minutes earlier.

'You implied my talents were a result of having a rich family.' She paused. 'You implied other journalists wouldn't have those talents unless they come from a rich family.'

'You're offended on behalf of other people?'

'It's called empathy. It's what makes me a damn good writer.'

And person.

She'd worked hard at that after her parents had all but abandoned her after the divorce. Granted, they hadn't been model parents before. Her mother had always been distant; her father an unyielding presence. That didn't stop her from trying to get their approval. Their love. A normal task for any child; a useless task for her. Her mother was travelling the world, living as though she had no child. Which was…fair. For all intents and purposes, Helen John *did* have no children. And Elena had no mother.

As for her father… Things were more complicated with him. The fact that he wanted her to marry someone for the sake of his business proved it. Especially when 'wanted' was a tame word to describe Cliff John's demands.

But indulging family issues wasn't professional.

'I…er… I shouldn't have said that,' she said.

Emotion flickered in his eyes. She had no idea what that emotion was, or why it felt dangerous. Alluring.

'I shouldn't have mentioned your family.'

'I'd appreciate it if you refrained from mentioning them again.'

The dangerous, alluring emotion flickered again. It gave her the distinct impression she was being toyed with. Everything inside her went on alert.

'Things aren't what they seem in the John family, then?'

She took a moment. Leaned forward. 'If you want to do this, Micah, you better be ready to do this. Because if my family isn't off-limits, neither is yours.'

A challenge.

Micah thought he'd learnt everything he needed to know about Elena during the interview portion of their conversation. She was sharp, insightful, compassionate. He wouldn't have thought her combative though. But how else could he interpret her challenge?

A fair response to you pushing the issue of her family?

That might have been it. Beyond wanting to know more about the John empire, he had no real reason to keep pushing. Did he *want* to provoke her, then? And if so, wasn't it fair for her to respond in kind? Except she wouldn't be able to if he didn't reveal how much of a sensitive topic his family was. He needed to pull back before he did.

This was part of why he never wanted to engage with people on more than simply a surface level. He didn't want to talk about his parents, or the distance they'd put into their relationship with him. He certainly didn't want to talk about his efforts to breach that distance. Efforts that had failed over and over again.

It made putting effort into any other relationship too exhausting to contemplate. So he didn't. Which wasn't entirely a problem since people who wanted relationships wanted to be engaged on more than a surface level. Even those who claimed they didn't want that. The women he dated always said they were fine with what he offered—at the beginning. As the months went by and he continued to dedicate himself to his business, to his relationship with his parents, they would express unhappiness. Eventually, they left. He no longer believed them when they said they wanted what he could give.

But he believed Elena. Believed that she would dig deeper into his family if he didn't stop her now. He couldn't afford to be intrigued by her. She might have been a puzzle of emotions he couldn't solve, but she was dangerous. He couldn't keep trying to put the pieces together, especially when he didn't have the full picture to work from. She wouldn't provide her picture, and he wouldn't provide his, and they would get along fine.

Why did that feel like a lie?

'I've already told you about my family,' he said, keeping his voice steady.

'You were "raised by a single mother, a lawyer with her own firm, and saw your father on occasion",' she recited. Tilted her head. 'Is that right?'

The side of his mouth tilted up. 'Yes.'

'That's what all the other articles about you said, too.' She pretended to examine her nails. 'It would be great to go into more detail. What was it like having a mother with her own law firm? Was it challenging? Inspiring? Did her success affect her relationship with your father? Did it affect yours?'

'Good,' he said after a beat. 'Great, in fact. Get all these questions out now, in the plane, so that when we get to Italy we don't have to waste time going through them.'

Her lips curved. 'Not fun, is it?'

It took him a moment. 'That was a trap.'

'It was and it wasn't,' she said easily. 'I would love to have that information for the article. But I also understand that you don't want it in the public realm. Because of my *empathy*.'

He studied her. Saw both triumph and sincerity on her face. She was slippery. Smart, too. He wasn't sure if he liked the combination. No—he wasn't sure what it meant that he *did* like the combination.

He didn't dwell on it. He needed to figure out what to do about her curiosity first. He didn't want to tell her the truth about his family. What would his parents say if they were included in an article about him? Would they even care?

His father had a brand-new family. Well, not new any more. His baby sister was twenty and his brother, seventeen. Regardless, his father had other things to worry about than what his thirty-two-year-old son said about him. Back when his father had had him, the idea of legitimacy still mattered. That was how his father had treated him. Like a mistake he didn't have to validate except on the rare occasion, when his guilt got the better of him.

And his mother? His mother would…not read the paper. She worked, hard, and that gave her little to no time for leisure. Elena had hit it on the head; his mother running her own law firm was both challenging and inspiring. But it was the inspiring part that mattered most. Perhaps, if he said something like that, Elena wouldn't speculate. And if his mother did ever see this, there would be no reason for her to be upset.

'Fine.' His tone was reluctant. Annoyed. He could see it in her smile. He cleared his throat. Hoped it cleared the emotion he didn't need her seeing. 'I'll answer one of your questions. We won't talk about family again after this.'

He didn't expect the agreement he got.

'Really?' he asked. 'It's that easy?'

'It's that easy,' she replied. There was nothing but sincerity in her tone now. 'I'm writing an article about you. I'm shadowing you for the next seven days to do so. None of that will work without a bit of give and take. From both of us.'

Those last words were heavy with implication. He barely refrained from rolling his eyes.

'We're in agreement, then. Family is off-limits?'

'Between me and you, yes,' she said brightly. 'I still want to offer my readers a good article.'

She'd told him he wasn't as charming as he thought; what would she think if he told her she was more charming than she could ever believe?

He stiffened at the thought. Told himself to get a grip. He was getting distracted from his plan. Elena herself—her personality, her looks, all of her—had already caused him to trip on some of the steps. But he would keep his goal in mind. That meant thinking clearly, strategically. No distractions.

'My mother is incredibly successful,' he said, keeping it concise. 'She worked hard, and was ready for the opportunities that came her way. That's what she taught me, too. To work hard and be ready. I did, and I was.'

'With Killian Leather and The Perfume Company?' she asked, naming the two clients he'd signed in the last year. Two of his biggest clients, who were part of the reason he'd been named Businessperson of the Year.

'Exactly.'

'She sounds like she inspired you.'

He tensed, but answered. 'She did.'

'Wonderful, thanks.' She switched off the phone he hadn't even realised she'd put on again. 'That was great.'

He nodded. Slowly let out the air that had been accumulating in his lungs. He'd survived it. He'd survived talking about his mother. Elena seemed content with his answer, which was great. She wouldn't ask any more. Or was he being naïve, believing her? He wasn't sure he would believe anyone else. But Elena was genuine in a way the other journalists he'd talked with hadn't been.

What if that was wishful thinking?

A sigh distracted him.

'What?' he asked.

'I can almost taste the steak.' She sank down

in her chair, closing her eyes. Her hair pushed forward, framing her face with thousands of curly strands. 'I'm going out on a limb here, but I bet there'll be fries with it. Maybe a mushroom sauce.' She looked at him. 'Am I right?'

He lifted a finger of one hand and picked up his phone with the other. He relayed Elena's suggestions to the chef, who grumbled as neither had been on his menu. But he agreed. Micah did pay him a significant amount of money for that agreement.

'Yes, you're right,' he said when he was done.

'You didn't have to do that.'

'What's the point of having a private chef when you can't do that?'

'It's so…privileged, isn't it?'

She spoke thoughtfully, giving him a clue that he shouldn't give the startled laugh he wanted to.

'I'm sorry,' he said after a moment. 'I have no idea how to respond to that.'

'You aren't that out of touch that you don't know people don't live like this.' She gestured around them.

'Of course not. I used to be one of those people.'

Her pensive expression deepened. 'Not entirely though. I can't imagine the mother that owned a law firm left you struggling in your life.'

'A lot of my mother's money went back into the firm.'

'Are you saying you grew up poor?'

'No, I'm not,' he answered immediately. 'And since I seem to be speaking to a reporter, let me clarify: all of this is off the record.'

She lifted her hands in surrender.

'I didn't grow up poor,' he said. 'I had enough. My needs were more than fulfilled.'

'But?'

'But...my wants weren't.'

He wasn't talking financially, though it was true. He hadn't ever had the courage to ask his mother for something he wanted. He didn't want to be a nuisance or a burden. He made do with what she gave him, even when it meant he didn't have the things he wanted. He couldn't exactly complain about that when he had everything he needed, could he?

'Your wants involved a private plane? Private chefs?'

'Elena,' he interrupted when she opened her mouth to add something else to his list of faults. 'Is there a reason you're interrogating me like this? I try to use my money in a way that makes me as efficient as I can be. I also spend a significant portion of that money trying to help other people. I have no doubt we'll speak about that in depth in the coming week. So, why are you judging me?'

'I'm not judging you.' She shook her head. 'This is all just…familiar. But at the same time, it's not. It's like déjà vu, except in reverse. This has happened to me before, and I remember that it did, but I can't… I *don't*… feel like it's real.'

Faint lines appeared between her brows. It was adorable. It was concerning that he found it adorable.

'You don't live a life of luxury any more?' He didn't expect her expression to turn to stone. 'Wait—you don't live like an heiress?'

'No.' She straightened. It was as effective as her putting up a shield. 'I gave up the private planes and chefs a while ago. I even left behind the gold cutlery, diamond plates, designer cell-phone covers.' Her eyes sparkled with challenge. 'It's been a tough transition, but somehow, I manage.'

He couldn't help the smile, but he didn't know what to say. The research his assistant had dug up on Elena seemed woefully inadequate now. Or did it? He hadn't gone through all of it. He hadn't had the time. But he'd read her entire portfolio. Noted her earlier articles weren't as good as her current ones. Her personal information hadn't seemed important to him. He wanted a path to her father, not a relationship. It was foolishly naïve of him not to realise the personal information would have given him a clue to whether she was the right path to her father.

In fact, now it seemed embarrassingly clear that she might not be in her father's good graces. She was an heiress to billions, yet she was working as a journalist for a newspaper. As many other people had, he'd thought this was a flight of fancy; an indulgence. But now he saw she needed the job. It was her livelihood. She loved it, clearly, but it made her sharpness, her growth, the offence she'd taken at him attributing skill to wealth more nuanced.

He wanted to know how that would affect his plans. But he also wanted to know why. Why was Elena supporting herself when her father could do so without feeling it?

He needed to read the rest of what his assistant had dug up on Elena. For research purposes. For his plan. That it would maybe answer his other questions about her was irrelevant. No, those *questions* were irrelevant. There was only the plan.

There could only be the plan.

CHAPTER THREE

ELENA WAS BEGINNING to realise Micah's intensity came in different forms. Amusement. Concern. Hesitance. Annoyance. She wanted to know what other forms there were. Would he be that intense in a romantic relationship? In a physical one? The thought turned her skin into gooseflesh. It was probably best not to examine why. Not that she needed to examine why. That was pretty clear.

She blew out a breath.

Entertaining her attraction to Micah was a bad idea. She knew it. Yet she still thought those inappropriate things about his intensity. And when he offered her the bed at the back of the plane to rest, she wanted to invite him to share it with her.

Maybe she had altitude sickness because she was on a plane. That was what that meant, right? She'd lost her ability to think clearly because of a lack of oxygen or something. Except she was still thinking clearly. She knew Micah's intensity was dangerous. His power was dangerous. Her father had both, and he used them without a thought of the consequences. Even if those consequences were people's lives. His daughter's life.

Marrying Jameson will ensure your security for the rest of your life. Even if, say, you happen to lose your job.

What he was really saying was that if she didn't marry Jameson, she would lose her job. Her security. After her father had used his money to control her for the first sixteen years of her life, she'd fought for her independence. Her job and security came because of *her* efforts. They had nothing to do with him. But she had no doubts he'd be able to strip away the fruits of those efforts. He was powerful enough that if he wanted, Elena would lose the job she loved. She would lose everything else she loved—her house, her car, herself—too.

She tried not to judge herself too harshly for considering her father's proposal then. She hated that she was, but she hated what would happen if she didn't give in, too. The entire situation turned her stomach. A work trip to

Italy gave her the perfect excuse to escape the constant loop of thinking about it. Or so she'd thought. She hadn't anticipated her reaction to Micah. She hadn't anticipated that he would use the same tactics her father had to get her here. But they were cut from the same cloth. If she allowed it, that cloth would wrap around her face and suffocate her.

She stood. She was feeling too restless to sleep. She'd let Micah have the bed for the next couple of hours, and she'd get a start on transcribing the interview she and Micah had had before the conversation had veered onto steak.

She slid through the doorway that separated the bedroom from the rest of the plane. Then she stopped. Micah was there, pacing the length of the space. His shirt was open from his neck to midway down his chest, as if he'd started to change but had forgotten. He had papers in his hand, and he looked down at them at various moments during the pacing, his lips moving. He was clearly practising something. Based on the shirt, the way he ran his hand over his face, practice was not going as he wanted.

'Do you want some help?'

He whirled around, his eyes wide, and Elena thought it might be the only time she'd see Micah unprepared.

'Holy smokes, you almost gave me a heart attack.'

'Holy smokes? *Holy smokes?*' She couldn't help the laugh. 'I thought you were, like, thirty? Thirty-year-olds don't say *holy smokes.*'

'I thought you were in your twenties,' he grumbled back. 'People in their twenties shouldn't wear unicorns.'

She looked down. Well, crap. She'd forgotten to change. She'd pulled on her favourite nightshirt when she climbed into bed. It was raggedy, admittedly, stretched so it fitted over her shoulders loosely, skimming her thighs. It was perfectly modest otherwise, and the vest top she wore under pressed her breasts to her chest so hopefully, they wouldn't give him an eyeful. She absolutely didn't want that.

She cleared her throat. 'Unicorns are a magical species that appear when you open yourself up to the possibility.'

There was the briefest pause.

'Are you saying I don't believe in unicorns so they've chosen not to appear to me?'

'I think that's a question you have to answer for yourself.'

Don't suffocate, her brain reminded her. Yes. Yes, that was important. Why did it feel as if she wanted to forget it?

'So—do you want me to help you practise whatever it is you're practising?'

'It's Italian. You wouldn't understand.'

'Oh, we're jumping right to the patronisation then.' She straightened from where she'd been leaning against the doorway. 'In that case, I guess you don't want my help.'

'No, wait.'

She hadn't moved. The fact that he thought she had—and how much power that implied she had—shimmered through her.

'Can you speak Italian?'

'I can, actually.'

'Seriously?'

'Micah, stop this. You're embarrassing yourself every time you underestimate me.' She walked to sit at the seat he'd been sitting in earlier, and curled her legs under her. 'Okay, first give me context.'

He lowered to the seat she'd been in earlier, bracing his forearms on his knees. 'I'm supposed to speak at this banquet once we arrive in Rome. It's in honour of our partnership with Vittoria, which is—'

'The handbag company there were whispers about you signing with. Congratulations. But please, continue.'

'Thank you.' But he gave her a *How did you know?* look. 'I have to say a couple of words. But my Italian is…basic. I had a translator help me, but I think I'm screwing up.'

She held out a hand for the paper he had, scanned through it when she got it.

'There's nothing wrong with this. It's quick, to the point. Passionate, even.'

'I don't want my speech to be passionate.'

'Relax. The Italians will love it.' She handed the paper back to him. 'I'm listening.'

And she did, without comment as he went through the quick, to the point, passionate words. By the end of it, she thought she might deserve a medal. He was butchering the longer words, words clearly unfamiliar to him, though the easier ones he went through seamlessly. She took the page again when he was done, ignoring his questions, and tried to fix some of the words that had seemed too complicated for him. When she gave it back, he sighed.

'I have to learn this now?'

'Only if you want to sound better than you currently do.' She shifted forward, putting her hands in her lap. 'You don't sound bad. Your peers will appreciate the effort, I'm sure.'

He gave her a dark look. 'You like having this kind of power over me.'

'Not over you, over everyone. Must be the wealthy world I lived in as a child.'

Now he pulled a face. It was all very animated. Too animated for the smooth, charming millionaire. He was clearly frustrated.

'Fine, I get it. I overstepped. No need to re-hash it.'

'Man, you cannot take being wrong.'

'I wasn't—' He stopped himself. Lifted the pages. 'Thank you for this.'

'You're welcome,' she said sweetly. Didn't move. When he stared at her, she shrugged. 'You don't want me to help you?'

'I'll call you in an hour.'

'Why? Just practise in front of me. I'll help you if you need it as you go along.'

He shook his head, giving her a forced chuckle as he did. 'I'm not doing that.'

'Why not?'

'You're going to make fun of me.'

'Me?' She put a hand to her chest. 'I would never.'

He didn't reply. She shook her head.

'You're serious? Okay, I promise not to make fun of you. I swear I don't deserve having to tell you that, but there you go. You have my reassurances nevertheless.'

'This is a very different side to you.'

'I can say the same about you.'

She'd already thought that. As for herself... He was right. She was relaxing into her personality, despite her own warnings to keep her guard up. She needed to stay professional. She needed to keep herself safe.

'I don't like it.'

'My side, or yours?'

His look was wry. 'Both.'

The way that made her smile told her staying safe was going to be hard work.

Micah had no idea how he could pay attention to what she said when he was still trying to get over the unicorn. But it wasn't *really* the unicorn. It was the body beneath the unicorn. Her legs, long and full, brown and possibly the best thing he'd seen in his life. Her shoulders, visible through the stretched material of her nightshirt. She wore a strappy top beneath the shirt, so he wasn't treated to the breasts he somehow knew would be free if she were home. Though the rest of the shirt was loose and gave him nothing else of her body, his own reacted.

Tightened, tingled, made him feel like a damn teenager with all the need. And now she was teasing him, helping him, seeing through him.

Seeing through him.

He didn't like it. Any of it.

'I'll practise. Let's practise.'

She gave a satisfied nod, her eyes displaying the same mood, and she took his breath away. The surprise of it didn't help either. He hadn't ever responded this way to anyone. The women he dated were always the same type. The women who moved in his circles. There was nothing wrong with those women; they simply weren't who interested him. It was easy to stay unattached from women who didn't interest him.

He'd learned from his father that attachments would put him in situations he didn't want to be in. Micah was his father's attachment, after all.

Whatever this was with Elena needed to stop.

'Are you going to start?' she asked.

'Yeah. Yes.'

He cleared his throat. Started saying what was on the page. It felt better now. More natural. He had no idea how she'd even known what would feel more natural coming out of his mouth. But he was grateful. He was grateful for her patience as he messed up, more times than he cared to admit. He liked the way she teased him as she corrected him, how there was no malice in anything she said. She wasn't making fun of him; he'd conflated the ease with which she talked to him with that. Maybe because he didn't know what banter looked like. What ease looked like. What friendship looked like.

He stopped at that thought. Erased the memory of it from his mind. There was no friendship. No attraction. *Nothing.* Hadn't he just told himself why there couldn't be?

'That sounds pretty good,' Elena said after what felt like the millionth time they ran through it. 'When do you have to do this?'

'Tomorrow evening.'

'Then you have about thirty or so hours to practise.' She sat back in the chair. 'Plenty of time to sound like a natural second-language speaker.'

'Second language? Not first language?'

She wrinkled her nose. 'I can't perform miracles in such a short space of time, sorry.'

He bit the inside of his lip to keep from smiling. 'If you had more time though, right?'

'Exactly.' She smiled. 'Seriously, you sound fine. Everyone there will love you.'

'You should be there.'

Immediately after he said it, he wished he could take it back. But then he saw her face. She…glowed was the best way he could describe it. It was like being in a dark room and having someone suddenly put on a light.

'I will be. Though I don't have this event on my itinerary.'

'That's strange.' Since he hadn't had Serena

put it on her itinerary, he was lying now, too. 'It should have been there.'

'Hmm.' She took a second. 'Well, then, if it should have been there…'

'I didn't realise you could speak Italian,' he added. 'It gives me another reason to have you there.'

'Another reason?' she asked. 'What's the first?'

'Er… I… You're writing a piece on me. Of course.' He swallowed. 'You should see this.'

'I will. I was just going to explore Rome anyway. It's my first time in Italy.'

'You speak Italian fluently and it's your first time?'

Her expression closed, shutting in the light along with it. 'I took it at school with some other languages. I thought I would need it for…' She trailed off.

'But you didn't?' he asked, even though it was clear what the answer would be.

'No.'

There was something so troubling in her tone that he didn't push. He wanted to. The fact that he did told him he was getting invested in…in *her*, he supposed. It wouldn't benefit either of them to continue down that path.

'We're landing soon,' he said. Smoothly, because he didn't care about troubling emotions.

'Oh. Okay.'

She looked lost for a moment. Vulnerable. He shifted his weight between his legs. Reminded himself that he didn't care.

He didn't care. He didn't care. He didn't care.

'I'll…er… I'll get changed.' She stood and walked towards the back of the plane.

You don't care. You don't care. You don't care.

'Are you all right?' he blurted out. Because he did care. No matter how much he wanted to believe otherwise. No matter how confused he was by it.

She stopped, only looking over her shoulder.

'Of course. I'm always all right.'

With that, she disappeared into the bedroom. Again, he told himself that he didn't care. This time, it was because she'd lied to him.

CHAPTER FOUR

As a rule, Elena tried not to be miserable in the morning. When her parents divorced, her father sent her to boarding school immediately. She'd fast learnt the value of mornings then. They were the only time of day she had in silence.

Her first year, she'd spent thinking about what she'd done wrong. Her father wouldn't have sent her away because of the divorce. She'd had nothing to do with that. It had nothing to do with *her*. Besides, she didn't bother her parents when she was home. Her efforts before—the tea or coffee she'd brought them; the baking she'd done; the dinners she'd made—had received ambivalent reactions at best, annoyance at worst. She was doing what the staff did. Did she expect recognition for that?

No, she'd expected love.

But as she'd grown older she'd realised that

wasn't the way to go. She'd shifted gears. Tried to excel at school, or in extracurricular activities, because those were things people noticed. If people noticed, her parents would be more likely to notice, too. Maybe they would finally be proud of her. They hadn't been. Though she'd come close, once, with her father. She'd 'bested' one of his business rivals' children by passing her school year at the top of her grade. She'd carried around the approval he'd shown in that brief moment when she'd told him for years.

She suspected recreating that moment motivated all her future efforts to please him. Like considering a marriage that would stifle her.

It was silly. She knew it. His approval had come shortly before he shipped her off to boarding school without any reasons. It meant nothing. His punishment, however, could irrevocably change her life. That was what could happen if she refused to get engaged. That was what *had* happened after the divorce, when she'd finally realised, courtesy of an innocent comment from a schoolmate, she was being sent away because she looked like her mother.

Her father wasn't punishing her; he was punishing her mother. Or maybe he was punishing her, too, because she reminded him of his failure. That was how people like her father thought. Relationships were either successful or they failed. For reasons completely outside the effort they put into the person they were in a relationship with or the relationship itself.

Micah probably thought that way, too. It was a good reminder. She couldn't let how adorably insecure he'd been with his speech ingratiate him with her heart.

Elena took a deep breath and tried to stay in the present. It was early, the sun just lighting the sky, and she was standing in front of St Peter's Square, staring. She didn't have any desire to do anything but stare. Or simply *be*.

The Vatican wasn't first on the list of what she wanted to see in Italy, but she had been walking and stopped because of the peace and quiet. The early hour meant she'd beat out most of the tourists. As she walked to the square, pigeons scurried around, searching for food. They did so in the square as well, more of them, and that was the most activity in the place.

Elena walked between the stone pillars on

the outer boundary of the square, wondering why they called it that when it was technically a circle. She imagined what it would be like when the Pope celebrated Mass there. She wandered aimlessly from one side of the square to the other. She took pictures, thinking about who she'd show them to. There were people in her life. People at the newspaper, mostly. Proximity friends.

It had been the same at school. Real friendships were hard work. Harder for someone like her. She'd experienced, more than once, people wanting to be her friend because of who she was. Those who didn't know her background almost always changed once they realised it. Once they realised she had money. When she started to refuse her father's money—it came at too high a cost—they treated her differently because now she had none. Kind of like how Micah had treated her once he realised she didn't live with her father's money.

Was that what he did?

She refused to dwell on the answer to that. She was in Italy. For work, yes, but this *being* wasn't work. She had the morning free because, according to Micah's itinerary, he had a business meeting until lunch. Most of the itinerary she received were hours blocked out for business meetings, actually. Which was fine. She didn't expect them to hang out as if they were *friends*.

But she did wonder why he wanted her in Italy if he was only going to spend meals with her. They could have done that in South Africa. She knew why the newspaper had agreed to send her to Italy though. She could watch him take over the world first-hand and take readers on that journey, too. It would hopefully lead to a boost in sales for the edition, which would make up the expenses of sending her on a seven-day trip to Italy.

Micah must have got involved to get the higher-ups to agree to that length of time. Most profiles, if they involved some sort of shadowing, were two or three days long. Why Micah got involved at all had been a question to her. She had her answer now. He wanted her to write about him because she was a John.

It couldn't be as simple as that, she knew. Still, she was intrigued by him. From a purely professional perspective. It was part of why she had woken up early that morning. She'd hoped to have breakfast with him, to ask him questions about his charity work, so she could get started on her article if she was bored. She had missed him, which didn't seem like a loss now that she was exploring. She certainly wasn't bored. In fact, she wanted to see more. And as she thought it, she noticed a group of passengers getting on a sightseeing bus some distance away.

She hurried towards them, but the bus had left by the time she got there. A couple of conversations later though, she had her own ticket to a different sightseeing bus. It was leaving in thirty minutes, so she ducked into a café while waiting. It was busy, clearly a place both tourists and residents visited. When she asked for a recommendation on a café speciality, she was offered hot chocolate. Literal, melted hot chocolate. By the end of it, she was convinced she was meant to live near a place that served the drink.

After a leisurely morning of sightseeing, she got off at a stop closest to where she was supposed to meet Micah for lunch. Or so she thought. Apparently, Rome had two streets named the same about thirty minutes from one another, and so she was thirty minutes late. She stumbled into the restaurant hot and sweaty.

'Oh, my word, I am so sorry.'

She wiped a hand over her forehead as she slid into the chair opposite Micah. He was watching her over his glass of champagne, looking cool and calm. Of course he looked cool and calm. He'd been in this air-conditioned restaurant for at least half an hour. She, on the other hand, must have looked like a troll. Maybe the look would have worked, had she had bright hair. But her boring brown hair would make her look like a troll without the mitigating cuteness.

'You're mad, aren't you?' she asked when he didn't reply. 'I'm sorry. I was on a bus, and I got off at the wrong stop, then I had to take a taxi to get here, which was ridiculously expensive, by the way, and—'

'Why didn't you just take the car I sent for you?' he interrupted her, his eyebrow quirking in a way she wouldn't have thought sexy on anyone else.

'The car? What car?'

'I sent a car to the hotel.'

'Ah.' A waiter arrived and poured her a glass of water. He disappeared as mysteriously. Or maybe not. She was too busy drinking the water to notice. 'That would have entailed being at the hotel, and, as I said, I was on a bus.'

'A bus.'

'Yes. Sightseeing,' she added brightly. 'It was wonderful seeing the city. The Colosseum is as gorgeous in real life as it is in pictures. From the outside, at least. I didn't see the inside because I didn't want to be late to this although I am now and what would it have mattered?'

'Elena,' he asked after a pause. 'Are you... uncomfortable by any chance?'

'I...' She faltered. Pressed a hand to her chest when she realised there was, indeed, a flutter of nerves congregating there. 'How did you know?'

His lips twitched. 'A hunch.'

She thought back over the last few minutes. 'Oh. It's because I was talking so much. Hmm. You're perceptive.' She emptied her glass of water before continuing. She was already speaking when the waiter refilled it and disappeared again. 'I hate being late. I hate contravening anything considered to be polite. Politeness was drilled into me for eighteen years. From the moment I was born, I'm sure, until I left school.'

'It sounds exhausting.'

His eyes were kinder than she'd seen before. Maybe that was why she said, 'It was. But it was part of being a John.'

'What happened when you left school?'

She barked out a laugh. 'A lot. This isn't about me, though I know you prefer it that way.' She let that linger. 'How was your meeting?'

He smiled, but not in a friendly way. It was satisfactory or knowing. It was also possibly both or something else entirely. The effect it had on her was distracting her from being able to tell. There was a fluttering in her chest and her skin was clammy. But then, she'd been late, and it was hot. Why did it increase after Micah smiled? She had no idea. She was considering an engagement to someone else. She shouldn't be noticing other men's smiles.

But she was. The wrong man's smile, because Micah wasn't a good match. He was too powerful, too intense, too distractingly handsome for her. It didn't matter though. What she felt for him was more than she'd ever felt for Jameson. Even though their marriage would be purely in name, that didn't sit right with her. Nor did the thought that Jameson would likely sate his physical needs with women outside their marriage. Heaven knew she didn't want to sleep with him, but she doubted he would be discreet about his relationships. How would that affect her as his wife?

'It went well,' he said, interrupting her panic. 'It was with the executive board of Vittoria. Just to iron out some details about the way forward.'

She waited as he gestured to the waiter, gave an order for a wine she would die to taste, before she asked her question.

'What does it feel like to be so successful in your thirties?'

She'd taken out her phone, pressed record while she'd been waiting for him to finish with the waiter.

'It feels...like a challenge.' He shrugged when she looked at him. 'It wasn't easy to gain success. It took ten years of eighteen-hour days, seven days a week. Most of the time, I pushed to see if I could. Now, of course, there's the pressure to continue being successful. Otherwise, I'm a fluke. It's a challenge.'

She leaned forward. 'That light in your eyes tells me you're up for it.'

Now his smile was catlike. 'I wouldn't be who I am, where I am, if I weren't.' There was a short pause. 'When people say "Do what you love and you'll never work a day in your life", I laugh. *Anything* you spend a significant amount of time on is work. Be that in your professional or personal life. The key is that when you find something you love doing, you won't mind putting in the work.' He sat back. 'Is that a good enough soundbite?'

She switched off her phone and mirrored his position. 'It would be an excellent soundbite—if I needed one. I don't. I'm writing about you.'

He narrowed his eyes. 'You know what I mean.'

She smiled. 'I do. But it's nice to see someone so easily confident get annoyed.'

'I wasn't annoyed.'

'I know.' But she smiled. Just in case it would annoy him.

He tilted his head, then shook it and laughed. 'You're something else, Elena.'

And you like it.

She startled herself. Those words were on the tip of her tongue. It sounded like...like *flirting*. She wasn't a flirt though. She chose her words carefully to avoid being one. Except in Micah's presence, apparently. Then, she spoke freely, and damn if that freedom didn't make her feel good.

'I took the liberty of discussing a menu for us with the chef, by the way,' Micah said. 'I thought it might be nice for you to experience full Italian dining.'

'Chefs must *love* you,' she said with a small laugh. 'Honestly, you realise you're not the only patron in this...'

She trailed off when she realised they were, indeed, alone.

He kept his eyes on her face as she realised it was only the two of them in the room. When she met his gaze, her confusion had the butterflies in his stomach scattering as if a stone had been thrown at them.

'There's no one here,' she said.

'I'm aware.'

She looked around again. What did she see? Sophistication in the wooden floors and accents throughout the restaurant? Class in the white and brown lines of the wallpaper on one of the walls, the brown and white paint on the others? Did she see romance in the white tablecloths, the candles adorning them? Or was it homeliness in the green leaves spilling over pot plants at strategic places; the framed pictures of the Italian family who'd created this wonderful place?

He'd seen all of it when he'd walked in an hour ago. He could do nothing about the décor, but he'd contemplated the candles. It was a warm summer's day outside. Why else would she think they needed candles?

For light, a voice in his head told him. He hadn't asked for the candles; they illuminated the darkness inside the restaurant. It wasn't overwhelmingly dark, but enough so that the candles were needed. He was probably being overly sensitive. He didn't need a waiter to tell him that. So he said nothing. Except now, as she looked around, he thought he should have.

'Two things,' she asked, her gaze meeting his.

He agreed with a nod. He couldn't speak because he was afraid of what his voice would sound like. Spellbound by how he'd just noticed the brown of her eyes were lined with some magical make-up thing. It made her eyes sparkle. It turned him into an idiot who indulged fantastical thoughts.

'One: do you own this place?'

'No.'

'Okay, then, two: did you do this for me?'

'I did it for us.' He stood now, walking to the bar where the waiter was standing and trying to be inconspicuous as he readied their wine. 'This place is usually closed this time of day, especially in the summer. I pulled some strings so we could have…lunch.'

He almost said privacy. That would have sounded dodgy. Luckily, the waiter offered him the wine to try. He went through the motions of tasting it, though it was one of his favourites and he didn't need to. With a nod of his head, Micah moved to Elena and offered her the glass. She did the same thing he had, but her eyes didn't leave his. He had no idea how drinking from the same glass could be erotic, but it was. Especially when Elena brought the glass to her lips, parted them, and he got the quickest glimpse of her tongue.

His blood got heavy, his skin grew tight, and heat spread through his body as if a fire had been lit inside him. Elena didn't help one bit. She was still staring at him with her beautiful brown eyes, her hair wild around her face, her lips red again, the colour mixing with the wine. The glass she offered him now had the trace of her lipstick on it, and it was the sexiest damn thing.

'Do you like it?' he asked, accepting the glass. It still had the tiniest bit of liquid in it, and he gave in to temptation by drinking it.

He placed his mouth on the outline of her lips.

'Yes.' Her voice was throaty. It did strange things to his body. 'Very much.'

The left side of his mouth lifted, and he lingered for much longer than he should have. But she was a magnet, and he was attracted to her, and he wanted, no, needed, to be as close to her as possible. Slowly, he turned around and walked to the bar.

'We're happy with this,' he told the waiter softly. The man gave him a knowing look, but it was gone before Micah could say something about it. All that was left was cool professionalism. Micah needed to follow his lead.

'Shall I get the starters ready, sir?'

'Please.'

He took the two glasses of wine the waiter poured to the table, offering Elena hers before settling in his chair.

'How was the sightseeing today?'

'You're deflecting,' she replied.

'From what?' he asked, because he was deflecting, but he didn't think she'd be straightforward about the chemistry that had happened between them.

Did chemistry happen? Or was it something two people experienced? Either way, they had it, they experienced it, and Micah wasn't happy about it. He had a plan. She was part of those plans. Except…suddenly that didn't feel right any more.

Maybe he *was* deflecting. Maybe he was deflecting so much he couldn't even tell what he was deflecting from.

'The fact that we're alone. You don't have to impress me.'

'I know.' Relief made him say the words with a smile. 'If it makes you feel any better, I had the restaurant for the meeting before this lunch, too.' He hadn't. This had been entirely for her, but he couldn't admit it now. She was entirely too observant and after the chemistry? He couldn't admit the truth, even though he hated lying.

'Really?' Did she deflate? Was he projecting? 'No wonder it went well, then.'

'It's part of it, I'm sure. Now, would you tell me about your day?'

She narrowed her eyes, as if she couldn't trust his interest in her. He was offended. Partly because she was right to distrust him—his plan included getting her comfortable with him. But that wasn't the reason he asked. He wanted to know about her day.

It disturbed him, the intensity he felt in that desire. He couldn't remember ever being interested in knowing about someone's day. Days seemed so mundane. When he spoke, even during small talk when things were supposed to be mundane, he asked about events. Events had purposes. The same couldn't be said for days. Wanting to know about Elena's day, wanting to know with an intensity? It rightfully worried him.

It didn't stop him from being engrossed in her descriptions.

'I don't know, Micah. I guess it could be because I haven't travelled in such a long time. Or that I'm here, one of the places I always wanted to visit.' The small smile on her face was an intimate glimpse into her mind. He tried to memorise it. 'It's wonderful. Every single thing. Even the pigeon who tried to bite my finger off when I tried to pet it.'

'You tried to pet a pigeon?'

Her cheeks pinkened. 'I know, I know. I got caught up in the magic!' she exclaimed, lifting her hands in front of her. Then she laughed. 'When I was standing in front of the Trevi Fountain, I was the main character of a fairy tale. I would have sung, if I could. Instead, I tried to pet a bird.' She laughed again, but this time, buried her face into her hands. 'I am such a dork.'

'Yes, you are.' When she looked up long

enough to stick her tongue out at him, he laughed. 'I like it, Elena. It's…refreshing.'

'Well, then, if it's refreshing.'

And she rolled her eyes. Damn if that wasn't refreshing, too.

CHAPTER FIVE

HAD SHE THOUGHT she was in a fairy tale before? She must have been confused. Standing in front of a beautiful fountain, seeing people throw coins into it and make wishes was magical, yes. But getting ready for a fancy event, a dress waiting for her in her room along with fairies who did hair and make-up? It was something from her past. So far in her past she found it surreal.

She caught her breath at the elegant black gown. The material was soft and glossy, simple and sophisticated. Micah intended on her wearing it as it was, she was sure, but she had the perfect necklace to go with it. It was bright and African, the yellow, black, red and green of it mixing in a pattern perfectly representing her home. Her make-up and hair were flawless, and when she looked at herself in the mirror, she barely recognised the woman looking back at her.

It had been over a decade since she'd felt so luxurious.

She took a deep breath, pushed back the memories that were still coated with pain. Looked in the mirror again. She wouldn't be the woman missing a life where she had never been enough. Contemplating a life where the things that fulfilled her were gone, regardless of what she decided to do about marrying Jameson. She would be the woman looking back at her. The African princess from some fairy tale she'd created in her mind. For one night, she could forget the rest and be that woman.

She felt like that woman when she walked into the passage of the hotel and found Micah waiting for her.

His eyes widened, and his lips parted to such an extent that she wondered if it counted as his jaw dropping. Colour flooded his skin. She didn't think he realised it, or knew that he was clenching and unclenching the hand that hung at his side. His other hand was in his pocket, and she would have bet everything she had that he was clenching his fist there, too.

He wasn't the only one stunned by the other's looks, though she hoped she was controlling her response more than he was. She would forgive herself if she wasn't. Every fairy-tale princess needed a dashing counterpart and damn if he didn't provide the perfect one.

He'd shaved since their lunch. Got his hair cut, too. It made his face look more angular, his cheekbones more visible, that jaw more defined. His tuxedo accentuated every line of his body—which was magnificent, the muscles and softness she thought he might be a combination of. She would never know without touching him, and suddenly she understood what Micah's fingers curling and uncurling meant. He was fighting against reaching out and touching her. Now, she was doing the same.

Her heart pumped a little harder, more erratically.

'You look…' He trailed off before looking at her. The intensity was there, and this time she knew it was admiration, and maybe desire. 'I don't even have the words for it, if I'm honest.'

'I'd accept nice,' she said, her fingers curling around the yellow clutch she'd stuffed her lipstick and phone into. The latter was for recording the evening's events. And ignoring the calls from her father's office. She hadn't made her decision yet. He would have to wait.

'You don't look nice though.'

She gave a surprised laugh. 'I think you're supposed to pretend, at the very least.'

'No. No,' he said again. 'I meant you look… more than nice.'

Her laugh was more genuine this time. 'Thank you.'

His smile was sheepish. 'I told you I didn't have the words.'

'But you have the smile. And the general look of a man who likes what he sees. It's enough.'

Their gazes locked, lingered. She felt something intimate crawl up her spine. Her skin turned to gooseflesh in response.

'I bought you a plain dress for a reason,' he said softly, taking a step closer. 'I should have known you would take something plain and turn it into something magnificent.'

'You should have,' she whispered. 'It's exactly what I intend on doing with the story I write about you.'

He grinned. It was free, unrestrained. *Sexy.*

She'd never seen him smile that way before. She felt as if she were seeing her dress for the first time again—that admiration, that longing—but more intense. As if she'd seen a million of those dresses at the same time. She had no idea what was happening to her, but she didn't care. She only cared about this man. The way he looked at her. The way he made her feel.

It wasn't how Jameson and her father made her feel. Small, vulnerable. Coerced. She'd met Jameson the day her father had called her to his office, outlining his plans for her life as if she had no say in it. Jameson had simply sat there, giving her a smile that was self-satisfied, though she was sure he thought he offered comfort. Her lungs had tightened. Her head had swirled. And she'd had to summon every ounce of strength to say she'd think about it. A month later, she was still thinking about it. Her time was running out, as her father's phone calls indicated.

But now, with Micah, everything felt different. Time was endless. She didn't feel small, and the vulnerability she was experiencing was *powerful*. She knew she had a choice here, standing in front of him. And that she'd made a mistake when she'd said he was just like her father.

He was more dangerous than her father. He made her feel strong. Desirable. Like a woman who wouldn't allow herself to be strong-armed into sacrificing her freedom for someone who wouldn't do the same for her.

'Micah,' she whispered, stuck in his gaze.

She all but felt him touching her. Her imagination made her shiver at the contact. She could only guess what would happen if he really did touch her.

'I know.'

He moved closer to her. Then swiftly, suddenly, she was pinned against the wall between his arms.

Micah was well aware that he was seducing Elena. He was as aware that it was a mistake. He had asked Serena to resend him Elena's personal information. In it had been plenty of clues to the state of her relationship with her father. Where she lived, how she lived. None of it came as a surprise after their conversations. What *did* come as a surprise was that she was about to announce her engagement. In a lavish party the day after they returned to South Africa.

As soon as he read it, he wanted to speak with her. Demand to know if it was the truth. But a cursory Internet search told him it was. It was the talk of every gossip site in South Africa. The elite of the elite had been invited. It soured his mood. Clung to his body as he got ready for a banquet he didn't feel like going to. Got heavier when he realised he shouldn't feel this way at all. He hardly knew the woman.

Then he saw her in her dress, and all rational thought flew from his mind, leaving only emotion. A possessiveness he only now recognised as the cause of his dark mood demanded he make her see that there was something between them. He fought against it, had managed enough to give her some harmless compliments. To tease. But something changed in her gaze, in her body, and fighting was no longer working.

Now they were pressed together against a wall.

There had been space between their bodies when he'd moved her there; there was none now. She arched against him, aligning their bodies so that he could feel how her breath was leaving her lungs in short, quick puffs. So she could feel how having her delightful, curvaceous body against his made him feel.

He didn't give a single damn.

'Elena,' he whispered, tracing the lips that she had painted red again. It made her lipstick smudge, and he had to resist the urge to press his mouth against the shadows of red. 'What are you doing to me?'

'Nothing.' Her hand touched his hip tentatively. Then her fingers sank into his flesh. It didn't matter that there were two layers of clothing between his skin and her hand. He felt the contact. Worried that he'd always feel the contact. 'I can't do anything to you, Micah.'

He stiffened, but didn't move. Couldn't move. He would despise himself for it later—for seducing her, for touching her, when she was someone else's—but he was caught in a spell. A curse. A curse that made the first woman he'd ever felt this way about be unavailable.

'Do you love him?'

She frowned. 'Who?'

'The man you're getting engaged to. St Clair.'

Her lashes fluttered seconds before the vulnerability that had been in her eyes when he'd first touched her disappeared. The heiress was back. He was a hundred per cent certain that the heiress wasn't who she was any more, but she was there nevertheless. She was there when she'd first boarded that plane, and she was here now.

It wouldn't have bothered him so much if he didn't know she wasn't the heiress. If he didn't know the heiress only came out when she felt threatened. He made her feel *threatened*.

He took a step back.

'I'm sorry. I shouldn't have…' He shook his head.

'No, I'm sorry. I just…' Her voice faded. She lifted a hand to her forehead, obscuring her gaze. 'You caught me off guard.'

'Because you're getting engaged.'

'Yes. No. I… I haven't decided yet.'

'You haven't—' He broke off. 'What the hell does that mean?'

When she looked at him, her gaze was dangerously blank. 'It means your background check didn't tell you everything.'

'I didn't need a background check. It's all over the Internet.'

Colour seeped from her face. 'What?'

She fumbled with her clutch purse, took out her phone, typed in hard, quick movements. He hadn't thought it possible, but she went paler as she read. Having just experienced the shock himself—though heaven only knew why *she* was shocked—he took a step forward. Her head snapped up, and the fire there kept him from moving any closer.

'You didn't know?' he asked carefully.

'That I'm announcing an engagement I haven't decided on when I get back? No,' she said in a cold voice. 'I didn't.'

CHAPTER SIX

HE WAS ON EDGE. He shouldn't have drunk all that coffee before his big speech. Then he remembered that he hadn't drunk any coffee that day. It wasn't caffeine making him jittery, but the entire incident with Elena. Her reaction had been…disturbing. Or maybe it was just nerves about his upcoming speech.

Yes, nerves. Not Elena.

He ordered a bottle of water at the bar and, when it arrived, guzzled it down like a man dying of thirst. It would make him need the bathroom, and was likely not a good idea, but he had to do something. He hadn't been this nervous since he'd…

Since he'd pitched his business to his mother.

Oh, great. This was exactly what he needed. A reminder of the woman who never thought he was good enough for anything, let alone a speech. He blew out a breath. That was a tad melodramatic. His mother thought he was a perfectly okay human being. She treated him as she would anyone else.

That had been a big part of his problem as a kid. He was *her* kid; he didn't want her to treat him as she would anyone else. But he hadn't realised that until one day, when he'd been nine or so, and she'd dragged him along to some benefit. It had only happened once in his life—she had no one to babysit him and even she wouldn't leave a nine-year-old alone—probably because she'd learnt her lesson and had back-up babysitters for her back-up babysitters. In any case, he'd gone with her, sat quietly at her table because he was so damn glad to spend time with her that he wouldn't do anything else, and watched her.

She'd smiled. At so many of her clients. She'd chatted and laughed and had turned into a person he hadn't recognised. And he realised what was wrong with their relationship: he hadn't given her an incentive to care about him. He was just her kid. She didn't love his father, or want a kid, so no wonder she didn't want him. But if he made her care? If he was important enough to make her care? Yeah, that would change things.

It had taken him two and a half decades to do it, but he finally had. Tonight was merely the beginning. One part of his plan to get his mother to notice him. Though the memories were painful, he needed them, and he was glad to have them.

So why was it Elena's face he sought in the crowd? Why did he feel confident and at ease because he looked at her? His mother was supposed to be his inspiration. Hell, he'd even take his father. What did it mean that Elena had burrowed her way into that plan?

Why did he feel guilty about the plans that involved her? And torn by the emotions he felt about her?

He set it aside and focused on his speech, which garnered him a rousing applause. He worked the crowd as he'd learnt to do over the years, before he realised Elena had disappeared. He gestured to Serena, told her to find Elena and bring her to him, and minutes later, she was at his side.

'Have you met Elena John, Lucca?' he said to the man he was speaking to from the executive committee for Vittoria. 'She's the reason I could deliver that speech this evening.'

Lucca exclaimed in delight. There were a few seconds of rapid conversation in Italian that he could barely follow, and then they were both laughing.

'Lucca says I should have let you make a fool of yourself,' Elena told him with a smile that didn't quite touch her eyes. 'He says I took away an opportunity for you to learn humility.'

'And you think I need it?' Micah asked in Italian. The bark of laughter he got in return told him all he needed to know. 'Well, now you have it,' he said good-naturedly.

Another quick sprint of Italian.

'You've endeared yourself to him,' Elena said.

'And it only took humiliation.'

'Do not worry,' Lucca said, patting him on the back. 'It happens to all of us at some time.'

'I sincerely hope to find it happening to you some time soon.'

Their laughter attracted a few more people, and before he knew it he was socialising with the executive committee of the company he'd just partnered with.

He had, of course, expected to chat with everyone. He hadn't expected socialising, with

wine and laughter and teasing. He'd never experienced any of it before, at any of the galas
he'd been to. He could have said it was the
Italians, who had a greater desire for jovial-
ity than his other business partners. It would
have been a lie though. The real difference
was Elena.

She switched between Italian and English
effortlessly, charmed easily, and ensured she
spoke with everyone at least once. This wasn't
her party—it wasn't even his—and he knew
she was still distracted by what happened earlier. But she'd claimed the role of hostess as if
it had been designed solely for her. He wanted
to speak with her, to thank her, to give her a
chance to breathe, but he couldn't get a second alone with her, she was so popular. In the
end, he gestured to her with his head, and left
the group under the guise of getting another
drink. She joined him in the foyer.

'Your business parties are exhausting.'

'They are for the life of the party.'

She shook her head. 'That's not a role I want,
nor deserve.'

'You might not want it, but you deserve it.'

He offered her his arm before she could reply. 'Can we go somewhere private to talk?'

Elena hesitated, her expression tightening. But she placed her hand on his. They walked over the soft blue carpet of the hotel's foyer to the elevator. Elena didn't say a word when he pressed the button for the roof. When they got up there, she gasped.

'Why didn't they have the banquet up here?'

He looked around. Glass gave them the perfect view of a night sky that was, in his opinion, showing off. Stars twinkled brightly above them, enticing people to stay outside, to pay attention to their beauty. Beneath them, Rome showed off as audaciously, lights sparkling, people moving, music thumping. It seemed that Rome's night life was more active than its day life, which he understood. It was summer, the night was slightly cooler, though by no means cool. It was the perfect weather for parties or dinners on a terrace.

It was the perfect weather for seduction, temptation. For making mistakes. Even the prospect had him shivering. He set the desire aside.

'Thank you. For what you did down there.'

'It was nothing.'

'No, it wasn't,' he said. 'You're the reason those executives are looking forward to working with me. I seem like a great guy.'

'You don't think you are?'

He opened his mouth, but discovered he had no answer.

When she realised it, she gave a small nod, then walked across the stone-coloured tiles that lined the pathways between the rooftop garden the hotel had created on one side of the room. The garden was mostly made of potted plants and flowers, though large trees full of green leaves peeked over those pots. The side of the room he was standing on had tables and chairs, and he wondered why they'd chosen not to integrate the two so it didn't feel so disjointed.

'I can't quite figure you out,' she said, facing him.

His breath did something odd—tightened, caught, gushed out of his lungs. He knew it was because she made a picture in her black dress, her necklace gleaming bright against her almost gold skin with the backdrop of greenery behind her.

'What do you want to know?' He would tell her anything.

'Is it always about business for you?'

The question was more serious than she let on, he knew.

'It has been for the last decade or so. Since I went to university.' He walked to the edge of the room, leaned his back against the glass. 'It's given me purpose.'

'I understand that.' She was quiet for a long time. 'My work's done the same for me.'

'For how long?'

Her eyebrow quirked. 'Since I turned sixteen.'

'You wanted to work since you were sixteen?'

'No. I found purpose in work when I was sixteen. That's when my parents got divorced.'

He didn't answer, only waited for more. She was walking before she spoke, her gait smooth, elegant, as if she walked runways instead of streets. Part of him wanted to blame it on her upbringing. Wealth made people believe the world was theirs to claim, much as models did the runway. But something deep inside him resisted. Her upbringing might have taught her that, but somewhere along the way she'd learned to earn the world, too. At least her part of it. Everything he knew about her from the last two days they'd spent together pointed to it.

'I'm not the kind of person who almost kisses another man when they're supposed to be engaged,' she said. 'I need you to know that.'

He studied her. 'Then what kind of person are you?'

Her mouth twisted. 'A pawn in a powerful man's game.'

'What do you mean?'

She wanted to close her eyes and sink to the floor. The evening had taken so much of her energy. As had discovering her father and Jameson had planned an engagement party and invited the entire world before she'd even given her answer.

Because they think they already know your answer.

And why wouldn't they? Her father was used to using his power over her as a bargaining tool in her life. His money, when she'd needed something at school and he'd tell her to attend some event in return. To pretend the divorce hadn't changed their perfect little family, even though her mother was halfway across the world. When she'd got a scholarship that paid for university and accommodation and she no longer needed his money, he began to use her need for his love. He'd promised a dinner, to accompany her to a social event, to put in a good word for her at a potential employer. She needed his approval so much she would accept anything from him, despite how terrible it made her feel after.

Because she was compromising to get it. Her values, her independence, herself. This latest request was the biggest, and her father was pulling out all the stops to get her to agree. Threatening her job, promising her security, implying his approval. It wasn't worth it, she knew, but it was tempting. She didn't want to lose the life she'd spent almost a decade building. She didn't want to lose her chance of her father ever truly loving her.

Now there was Micah, complicating it all with his power over her. Because he had some. Why else was she there, trying to explain herself to him? Why else did she still want to kiss him? To let him hold her and make *her* feel powerful again?

It was a trap. It couldn't be anything else. And it was bound to make her feel as terrible as giving in to her father did.

'You're a powerful man, Micah. You know you play games. Use people.'

Anything she could have read on his face was covered by a blank expression. 'I don't know what you're talking about.'

That wasn't the reaction she had expected. She'd expected denial, or confusion. Genuine confusion, not this practised nonsense he was going for.

An uncomfortable feeling slithered down her spine. It hissed in her ears, saying *I told you so.*

'What are you hiding?' she asked softly.

'I'm not hiding anything.'

'Yes, you are.' She took a step closer. 'And it has to do with me.'

He didn't reply, only watched her with a guarded expression. She blinked, and stumbled back. It *did* have something to do with her. And if she took the rest of the conversation into account, it meant he was using her, too. But for what?

It didn't matter. The only thing that did was knowing she couldn't trust him.

She hated that it sent a crack rippling through her heart.

CHAPTER SEVEN

ELENA'S SECOND FULL day in Rome wasn't as exciting as the first. She spent the majority of it tailing Micah to his meetings. She'd expected it—that was what had been on the itinerary, and Serena had invited her to join him—and she'd brought her observation A game. She was quiet, discreet, and only spoke when spoken to. She was doing exceedingly well, actually, which was why Micah's stony expression whenever he spoke to her annoyed the hell out of her.

Actually, no. The real reason she was annoyed was because he was treating her as if *she* were the one keeping secrets. And she was sure it wasn't only keeping secrets either. His reaction to her questions the night before told her there was more there. She had set it aside though. She was a professional, after all. Except him showing everyone his disapproval of her made them both look *unprofessional*. She would have told him that, too, if she'd had any time alone with him that day.

But his meetings were back to back. When they had to change venues, they went in different cars, something she was sure he'd arranged. All of it made her annoyance grow. She stewed in it. Plotted her revenge. It wouldn't be sophisticated, but it would be satisfying. Like throwing her tablet at Micah. She would love to see his expression after that. But logic told her tablets were expensive—and so was Micah—so she settled for fantasising about his defeat instead.

They were supposed to have dinner at the end of the day, but Elena ducked out of it. She didn't want to socialise with him. She'd got enough information on his business habits during that day to write her article. Serena had sent her information about his charity work, and with the personal information Elena had got on the plane and in the restaurant, she could write a decent article. A *good* article. She didn't have to spend any more time with him. She relished that.

Her phone rang. Her finger hovered over the denial button, but it was Jameson calling now, not her father's office. He was the lesser of the evils. Besides, she had some things to say to him now that she'd processed the news of the party a bit more.

'Where have you been?' he said as soon as she picked up. 'We've been trying to get a hold of you.'

'Hello, Jameson. How are you?'

'Busy. Work and…' There was a pause. 'Stuff.'

'Yes, *stuff*,' she said slowly. 'Like the party you and my father are planning to announce our engagement at?'

'Elena—'

'It's a little presumptuous, don't you think?' she continued, ignoring what would surely be some form of manipulation. 'Or is it strategic? I'm not in the country, so you can plan your party without my protests.'

'Elena.' Jameson's voice was sharp now. 'Your hysteria is helping no one. Calm down.'

She almost swore at him. Barely caught the words before they jumped from her lips.

'We were merely moving things forward.'

'Moving me forward, you mean.'

'Your father assured me your answer would be in the affirmative.'

'I'm sure he did,' she murmured, her anger changing from sharp heat to something…cold. 'Is that why he's been trying to get a hold of me, then?'

'Having confirmation from you would be helpful.'

Not to me.

So say no, another voice said in her head.

And she wanted to listen to it. She wanted to say those words. But they wouldn't leave her lips, no matter how hard she tried. Something entirely different came out instead.

'I'm working,' she said woodenly. 'So you'll have to wait a little longer for that confirmation.'

He cursed. 'You're prioritising that man over me? Your future husband?'

'It's not about a man.' *And you might not be my husband.* 'It's about my job, and the fact that anyone could have got this assignment, but they gave it to me.'

'They gave it to you because you're a John. You don't have to prove yourself, if that's why you're doing this. You already have.'

She didn't bother to reply. Jameson would think that her worth was solely in her surname. It made Micah's assumption of the same on the day they met worse. She didn't indulge her thoughts about why that was. Accepted that she was raw when it came to Micah and left it at that.

'It's not a huge leap to assume Williams asked for you,' Jameson continued, apparently not caring that she hadn't responded. Though the way he hit the nail on the head felt like a whip against her heart. 'He probably thinks you're his key to partnering with the John Diamond Company.' Jameson laughed. 'Our engagement will secure my and your family's partnership though, so he'll quickly realise having you there was for nothing.'

For one horrifying moment, she thought she would gasp. Her head swirled, and she stumbled back to the bed, lowering so she had support for the knees that had gone shaky.

'Elena? Are you there?'

Her training kicked in. The sixteen years before the life she knew had fallen apart consisted of her parents coaching her in the art of vulnerability. That was, to never be vulnerable. People would use it against her. Powerful people would use it against her.

Micah had used it against her.

'Well, this has been lovely,' she said, her voice sounding odd, even to herself. 'We're travelling to the country tomorrow, so I'll be out of cell-phone range. Goodbye.'

She put down the phone before he could reply. She was about to switch it off for good measure when she saw a message from Micah.

Are you okay?

No. She wasn't okay. But she sure as hell wasn't going to admit that to a man who was using her. Just like every other man in her life.

What had she done to deserve this? To deserve feeling this alone?

She gave herself a few minutes to wallow, then went to her laptop to write.

Elena was waiting for him at breakfast. She wore a pink headband, curls spiralling around her head behind it, along with a pants suit—black this time—and a top that matched the headband. Her lips were painted the same soft colour, but she wore no other make-up that he could see.

She looked up when he arrived, took her cell phone out, pressed some buttons, then put it away.

'I emailed you the story I plan on submitting to my editor. It's only due when I get back, so feel free to add your comments and email them to me before the end of the trip. I'll apply them if they're reasonable,' she added with a warning glance.

'You're done?'

'I was inspired last night.' Her tone was flat.

'Serena told me you had a headache. That's why you didn't come to dinner.'

'I lied. I didn't come to dinner because you acted like a jerk the entire day. I didn't want to experience that for any longer than I had to.' She stood. 'Thank you for the opportunity to—'

'Wait,' he said, standing out of surprise. 'You're leaving?'

'I am.' Her spine straightened, as if she was daring him to argue with her. 'I'm going to Venice.'

'Why?'

'A number of reasons. None of which,' she added as he was about to ask, 'I'd like to share with you.'

'Okay, wait. Just…give me a second to catch up.' He looked around desperately. 'Coffee? Let's have one coffee together.'

Her expression was emotionless. 'Your driver is standing in the doorway, Mr Williams. If I remember correctly, your meeting starts in thirty minutes.'

'Elena,' he said sternly now. He softened his tone when her eyebrow rose. 'I'm sorry. Just… please. Coffee?'

He didn't know how long he waited for her to give the nod that eventually came. All he knew was he was offering to get coffee for them, even though a server could have done it. But he needed time to process. To ask himself why he hadn't expected her to stand up for herself. Why he'd wasted a day that he could have spent with her.

His emotions. He didn't know how to work through them. They'd shared a tense almost kiss; he'd seen her fit seamlessly into his world; and he'd discovered she was about to be engaged. He hadn't been prepared for any of it. Then she'd come dangerously close to figuring out his plan and his instincts had told him to shut down. To protect himself. So he did. He'd spent an entire day trying to ignore her and being unable to because she was so damn vibrant and beautiful and he was pulled to her in a way he couldn't understand.

Damn his parents, he thought suddenly, un-expectedly, *furiously.* If they hadn't all but abandoned him, if they'd taught him how to engage with people, he wouldn't feel so lost now. He would know what to do with his feelings. He'd be able to deal with them in healthy ways. He wouldn't have sulked at Elena like a teenager because he liked her and didn't want to.

He liked her.

Coffee slopped over the cup onto his hand, burning his skin much as that realisation burnt his heart. He set the mug down, gritted his teeth, though a part of him wanted to brace over the counter. But he wasn't helpless; he could handle some feelings. With that thought, he refilled the liquid that'd spilled onto his hand, grabbed the other mug and went back to his table.

Elena didn't speak, only watched him as she accepted the coffee, bringing it to her lips immediately.

He swallowed. 'Elena—'

Her sigh cut him off. His eyebrows lifted before he could stop them.

'I'm sorry, did my voice annoy you?'

She didn't even pretend. 'I don't want an apology from you, Micah, which I can already see on your face is what you were planning on saying. I want to catch my train to Venice. I want to watch the green fields through the windows and enjoy the peace of not arguing with you.'

He studied her. There was something more going on.

'This is why you didn't reply to my message yesterday, isn't it?' he asked quietly. 'You're not okay.'

She closed her eyes. When she opened them, he sat back. He needed the support of his chair to understand what he saw there.

'No, I'm not okay. But you're part of the reason I'm not, Micah, so I don't have any desire to talk to you about it.'

CHAPTER EIGHT

IT PROBABLY HADN'T been her best idea to accept Micah's offer of coffee. Not when she was obviously in a fragile state—why else hadn't she controlled her tongue?

Oh, right. That look of complete and utter anguish on his face.

'You won't let me apologise,' he said, his voice low.

'Do you know what you're apologising for?'

His brow knitted. 'Yesterday. For acting like an inconsiderate, stubborn—' He exhaled. 'I was wrong yesterday.'

'What about the day before?' she asked. 'When you claimed you weren't hiding anything?'

His lips parted, but he didn't say anything.

'That's why I didn't want your apologies,' she said, pushing her chair back so she could stand. 'They don't mean a thing.'

'Elena—'

'No!' She slammed a hand on the table. 'I don't want to hear your excuses. I just want the truth. Did you or did you not bring me here because you want a partnership with my father?'

When he stared at her, the little hope she had that Jameson had been incorrectly speculating fluttered away, disappearing in the wind.

'Micah,' she said on what sounded like a hiccup, but couldn't be. That would involve having emotions about the situation. But she'd prepared herself for this, so, obviously, she had no emotions whatsoever.

'I was going to tell you,' he said softly.

'Were you?'

'I…' He paused. 'Not if I didn't have to, no.'

She pressed her lips together and tried to control the emotions she did, apparently, have. Control was better than feeling them. That swirl of disappointment and betrayal that made no sense when she'd known this man for days. When she was, essentially, working with him.

'I didn't think it would come to this,' he continued in that same soft voice. 'I didn't expect for us to…' He frowned. 'I only wanted you to introduce us.' The frown deepened. 'You shouldn't have been hurt by this.'

But I am.

She didn't say it.

'You could have found a million other ways to be introduced to my father,' she pointed out, proud of how steady her voice was. 'You could probably contact him now and he'd agree to meet with you.'

'I've tried that.' Despite his frown, the sternness he spoke with, he seemed vulnerable. Why did *he* seem vulnerable when he was the one with all the power? 'I wasn't as successful then. He wouldn't take a meeting with me.'

'He will now.'

'How do you know?'

She gave a mirthless laugh. 'If Jameson knows about you, my father knows about you.'

'Jameson… Your fiancé?'

The repressed emotion in his voice had her pressing the heels of her hands into her eyes. This was…a lot to deal with. At least she hadn't put on eye make-up that morning. She'd been too tired. All the effort she'd been able to muster was to put something on her lips to distract from the rings around her eyes. She was aware that wasn't how make-up worked, but it was the best she could do.

She dropped her hands. 'He's not my fiancé. He's just the man my father wants me to marry to strengthen his company.'

'What? *What?*'

The outrage almost amused her.

'I'm a pawn to him,' she said simply. 'Not unlike how you intended on using me for an introduction.'

'That's not… It's not the same.'

She only looked at him.

'Elena, my intentions weren't malicious. I promise. I was just…' He took a deep breath. Then he met her eyes. Fierceness had woven itself between vulnerability, the result so captivating she couldn't look away. 'You're right. I should have tried to get in contact with your father through other means. But I was afraid that…that my mother would find out.'

'Your mother?'

'John Diamond Company is a client of hers.' He was continuing before she had time to process that. 'Partnering with your father has little to do with my business, and everything to do with her. We… We don't have a relationship. I was hoping to change that.' The pause before he went on this time was longer. 'But if she thinks I orchestrated this, the chances of that happening…' He shook his head. 'She wouldn't appreciate being manipulated.'

'I can understand that,' Elena said bluntly.

He nodded. 'That's fair. But… This is how I do business. I make plans. I follow them. I don't think about the people involved.'

'That sounds callous.'

His jaw jutted out. 'It is.' He paused. 'I thought about you.'

She wanted to believe him, but… 'Did that change how you treated me?'

'It made things more complicated.' He sighed. Continued speaking as if releasing the breath had also expelled his resistance. 'I struggled with it. That's what happened yesterday. Among other things.' His fingers curled into a fist. 'It's easier to pretend not to know how my plans affect other people. For many reasons. Most of all because being callous makes me—'

'Like my father,' she cut in.

'I was going to say like my mother.' He heaved out another sigh. 'I don't entirely know how I feel about that. I'm working through some things.'

'Clearly.'

The side of his mouth lifted. 'You seem to be, too, with your father.' He paused. 'He really expects you to marry this guy? Say no.'

'Easier said than done.'

'Isn't there someone who can intervene?' he asked. 'Your mother?'

'I haven't spoken to my mother since my parents divorced when I was sixteen.'

Surprised fluttered over his face. 'I'm sorry.'

'Don't be. We didn't have much of a relationship before. I wasn't losing out.'

'But...she's your mother.'

'That doesn't mean much if she doesn't want to be my mother.'

'But—'

She interrupted him before he could ask more intrusive questions.

'If you'd just told me you wanted to meet my father, things would have been a lot easier. Instead, you were manipulative. And now I'm wondering things like if I'm good enough at my job to be here.' *Or if anything that happened between us was real.* 'I don't even know if I should trust anything you say. Are you telling me about your mother because you want me to understand your motivations? Or are you doing it for some calculating reason I'll only discover once I trust you again? I won't do that to myself.'

She stood. 'Send me your opinions on the article if you want. Otherwise, I'll see you on the flight home.' She didn't look back when she left.

It took him the rest of the day to clear his schedule. Micah did it without hesitation. There was a high likelihood the executive committee of his company would have something to say about that, but he could afford to ignore them this time. He'd brought in several high-profile clients over the last year. And if he got John Diamond Company—

He stopped. It was exactly that kind of thinking that got him into trouble. Admittedly, it was hard to shut down. He was used to methodical thinking. He'd been practising it for over a decade. Probably before that if he was truly examining things.

His mother was an excellent businessperson. Sharp, motivated, strategic. He witnessed these characteristics before he could describe what they were, especially when she used them on him. There weren't many traditionally maternal things about his mother. She spoke to him as if speaking to an employee. If the employee was an intern. Or someone she didn't want to deal with but had to.

The easiest way of processing it was if he responded in the way she treated him. She'd appreciated that, in that she hadn't looked too annoyed at him. In fact, the more he became like her, the less annoyed she was at him. But she also appreciated creativity, a fact he'd come to know after he'd written an essay at school about what he wanted to be when he grew up. He'd got an A for the essay, had shown it to her proudly. After one look, she'd said, 'Micah, you don't have the skills to become a lawyer.' He'd never learnt what skills she thought that was. 'Show a little creativity.'

And so his trajectory had changed. When he was old enough to figure out where it was headed to, he did research. On the kinds of clients his mother represented, on the kind of business she appreciated. It led him to the affluent market, and soon he'd seen a path to getting what he wanted. He happened to be damn good at it, too.

He was less good at relationships. Turned out the characteristics his mother had inadvertently taught him—the ones that made him so successful—didn't work as well in his personal life. He should have known. His mother hadn't been there for him at all. Nor for his father, which was part of why things hadn't worked out between them. That was based on his father's point of view, which he'd been privy to before his father had married and started a family with someone else.

The one significant thing about his father's marriage was that it showed Micah there was hope relationships could work. He'd never cared about that before. He struggled with the fact that he cared about it now. But he did. He cared that he'd hurt Elena. That she thought he was like her father, who wanted to use her as though she weren't a person. That he was like the man who would accept her as his wife, but thought of her in the same way.

He didn't understand relationships, but he knew he wanted more for Elena. He wanted more *with* Elena. She was the first person in his life to make him feel…things. He would accept being her friend if that was the only relationship they could have. But he needed to prove that she could trust him first.

Which was why he was now walking the narrow paths of Venice to his hotel. Elena had told Serena where she would be staying and had given her all the relevant contact details. It had taken some convincing—unsurprisingly, Elena had inspired loyalty in the woman that had worked for him his entire career—but his assistant had got him a booking at the same hotel. He had no idea if Elena was out exploring, or if she was dining at the hotel's restaurant, or if she was simply sleeping. But he had to take a chance, and hope he hadn't crossed a line by coming to see her.

After he booked in, he called her cell. She didn't answer. He rolled his eyes. His annoyance was both because she hadn't answered and because he'd expected her not to. He sent her a message.

I need a moment of your time, please.

He got a reply within seconds.

You had a moment of my time this morning.

He could picture her saying it, her lips pressed against one another, her eyes daring him to contradict her. For some inexplicable reason, it made him smile.

We both know this morning didn't go well.

Whose fault is that?

His smile widened. He probably looked like a fool, standing in the foyer, staring at his phone and smiling. He didn't care.

Mine. That's why I'd like to apologise.

I don't want apologies.

You deserve them.

There was some time before the next message came.

I'm not answering your calls.

You don't have to. Just tell me your room number and we can talk in person.

What?

No.

You're not here?

Those three messages came in quick succession.

Give me your room number and check for yourself.

His bottom lip curled beneath the top row of his teeth as he waited for her to reply. He knew it was impossible, but he wondered if she knew how hard his heart was beating and was punishing him. But that didn't seem like Elena's style. She seemed more like the physical torture kind, not the psychological one.

As if confirming it, her message came.

Room 542

He almost ran to the elevator before he realised he'd refused the porter so he could contact Elena. In hindsight, he should have only contacted her after he was settled. But Elena was angry at him, and it felt as if a sword were waiting above his head. It made no sense. It didn't have to. He would explain himself to Elena soon and that feeling would go away.

Ten minutes later, he'd thrown his bags into his room and was knocking on the door of room 542. An elderly lady answered.

'Well,' she said, after scanning him up and down. 'I didn't expect this as room service, but I can hardly complain.'

'Oh.' It took him a beat to realise Elena had duped him. 'No, ma'am, I'm sorry. This isn't—'

'Did you just call me ma'am?' Her accent became more pronounced.

'Yes. I'm sorry. It's something we use out of respect for—' He cut himself off. They didn't need to go into detail about what older women were called in South Africa. 'I'm not from here. Customs aren't the same. Please accept my apology.'

'You do like to apologise, don't you?' came a drawl from opposite them.

He glanced back to see Elena leaning against a doorframe with folded arms. Her hair was piled at the top of her head, her skim gleaming with what he assumed was sunblock, though it was evening and he was probably wrong.

His brain quickly noted the other things about her—she wore a sun dress, lilac and simple, and nothing on her feet—before he shifted.

'There you are, darling.' He kept his tone even. 'I forgot my key card and went to the wrong room.'

'It must be because of all the alcohol you drank at the parade,' she said easily.

'Getting locked out of my room quickly sobered me up,' he replied dryly, then turned his attention to the older woman. 'I'm sorry for disturbing you, ma'am.'

She didn't reply, only shut the door in his face. What would it have been like if he'd gone into her room for what she'd wanted? He shuddered.

'If you're cold, you should probably go inside.'

He turned. Noted her expression. 'You mean of my own room.'

'I do.' She smiled at him. It wasn't friendly. 'I have to admit when I didn't see you through the peephole after five minutes I thought you were lying.'

'That's why you told me the wrong room number?'

'No. I told you the wrong room number because I thought it would be funny.'

'Hilarious.'

Her smile was full of amusement now. 'Oh, I know.' There was a short silence after she sobered. 'What are you doing here, Micah?'

'I prefer not talking about this in the passage. Where I'm sure we have some eyes. And ears,' he added, easily picturing the woman who'd slammed the door on him eavesdropping.

'I prefer not talking about this at all, yet here we are.'

She wasn't going to make this easy, then. Okay. He expected as much.

'Can I come in? Please? Please,' he said again, for good measure.

She gave him a wary look, but stepped back to let him in.

CHAPTER NINE

SHE WAS EITHER the biggest fool in the world, or a sucker for a man who was prepared to grovel. Perhaps both. Probably both, she thought, as she stepped aside for Micah. Both, she confirmed when he walked past her and politely waited for her to close the door before he did anything else.

Both for him, a voice whispered in her head.

She shouldn't have answered his messages, or told him where to find her, or let him into her room. He put her in danger. He *was* danger.

'Your room is nice.'

'It's generic and dark, but clean and comfortable. I don't know if that qualifies as nice.' She sat on the bed. 'You didn't come here to compliment my room though.'

'No.'

He shifted, revealing his nerves. She shouldn't

have used the opportunity to check him out. He wore jeans despite the heat, though he was dressed the most casually she'd ever seen; he'd replaced his usual shirt with a T-shirt. It was tight over a body that looked muscular, but had the softness of someone who had been buff once, but didn't get to the gym as much any more. She had no idea whether that was true, or whether Micah's body simply looked like that.

What she did know was that she wanted to run her hands over his broad shoulders, down the firm rounding of his torso, back up. She wanted to kiss the crook of his neck and make her way down to the firmness of his bicep. She wanted to—

She closed her eyes. She didn't need this attraction. It only reminded her that she couldn't afford to share it with Micah. She didn't trust him. But it also forced her to think about the decision she had to make. How could she marry Jameson when she felt this way about another man? Would she indulge in an extramarital relationship as he no doubt would? The very thought of it made her uncomfortable. And she doubted Micah would want a relationship with a married woman anyway.

She shook her head. She shouldn't be thinking about this.

'Sit down, Micah,' she said softly. 'You're making me nervous.'

'At least we'll be on equal ground, then,' he muttered, but sat. 'So… I'm…er… I'm sorry.' It was so sincere she didn't even feel tempted to interrupt the apology. 'For everything, but mostly because I made you feel used. That… sickens me.'

She looked at him for a long time. Saw that he was telling the truth. It shifted something in her brain. In her heart. 'Thank you,' she said.

Her acceptance drew a frown, but he nodded. Then blew out a breath. 'I'd like to tell you why I did all this. Please.'

'Okay.'

'I've just…never spoken to anyone about it before.'

She resisted taking his hand. Resisted comforting him. It took more strength than she would have liked. 'When you're ready.'

After another nod and a breath, he began.

'My parents never married. They were dating while at university, found out they were having me, had me. They were about to graduate and they weren't meant to be serious. My mom already had a law firm she was going to do her articles at, and when they wanted to drop her because of her pregnancy, she threatened to sue them. They played nice, and she worked her butt off while my dad looked after me.'

He stood.

'They weren't happy together, but the arrangement worked for them, especially since my dad wasn't working and my mom was. But my mom was never home, and my dad realised he wanted more from life. When I was seven, they broke up for real. It was fine for my mom because she had a good job by then and she could send me to a school. My dad got a job of his own, and every semblance of family I had ended.' He walked to her fridge, took a bottle of water out. After he downed it, he said, 'I'll pay for it.'

She didn't care about that. She did care about the sad look in his eyes. It wasn't obvious. There was a resignation as he told the story, as if he were recounting something he'd told a million times before. Now she knew why he was so tight-lipped about his family. She also knew him telling her this was… significant.

'My point is,' he said suddenly, speaking fast, 'I don't know how to treat people.'

'You not having a family means you don't know how to treat people?'

'No.' He exhaled irritably. She preferred it to the sadness. 'It means I don't know… It means,' he said more deliberately, 'people are hard for me. Relationships are hard for me.'

'Who said anything about a relationship?'

'I didn't mean a *relationship*.'

'That's wh—'

'I know that's what I said,' he interrupted curtly. Exhaled. 'My mother raised me. But what she did wasn't really raising. I had food on the table, shelter, but I didn't have anything else. So, I followed my mother's example. I… I shut down the emotions. I was efficient and had single-minded focus.'

'That's why you're so successful,' she murmured.

'Yes.' He didn't blink an eye. 'But apparently, those characteristics don't do well when you're trying to befriend someone.'

Her lips curved. 'You're trying to befriend me?'

He heaved out a sigh and sat down next to her. 'Do you think I came here simply to torture myself?'

She thought for a moment. 'Thank you for coming here. For being honest.'

'I'm trying.'

'So I see.' Emotion swelled in her chest. She cleared her throat. 'I don't like being used.'

'I understand why.' He gave her another one of his intense looks. 'Does your father really expect you to marry for his business?'

She stood and walked to the window. 'Yes.'

'Will you?'

She didn't answer him for a long time. 'I don't know.'

Her considering marriage at her father's behest still sounded like a fantasy. It didn't belong in the real world. It didn't belong in *her* world. She was determined, independent, strong.

Why would someone like that put themselves in that position?

'Why?' he asked eventually. He needed to know.

'It's a difficult decision.'

'You know that's not what I meant.'

She sighed, but didn't answer him. He stood and joined her at the window. It was night, and all they could see were shadows below them. Occasionally, the light from someone's cell phone would come along and given them glimpses of outlines of faces and walls and cobbled stones. But Micah wasn't paying attention to that. He was looking at Elena.

The light in her room was bright and clear, allowing him to see every nuance of her expression. Naked emotions stalked across her face leisurely, as if it were a hot summer's day and they were prancing around the pool. She didn't try to hide them, and he could see the battle between guardedness and a desire to tell him. She met his gaze, but didn't speak. The rawness in her eyes made him want to pull her into his arms and tell her it was okay. She would be okay.

'We don't speak much these days,' she

started. 'Me and my father, I mean. Contact mostly came from me, anyway, and when I got old enough for self-preservation to win out over my desire to...' She trailed off. 'Anyway, he called me to his office. He never did that, and there was just this...hope inside me. Foolish,' she scoffed at herself. 'He wouldn't call me to his office to apologise for the years of neglect or for using me when he needed me. He only called to use me again.'

She leaned back against the window frame, her gaze now shifting to outside. 'When I got there, he told me about a mining accident that had killed two John employees. I already knew, of course. It was all over the news and it's my job to know the news.' She dropped his hand and folded her arms. 'He said stock was tanking and he needed something else for the media to focus on. And he'd found a way.'

'Marriage.'

She gave a curt nod. 'To the heir to a rival mining company. The company would be strengthened because of the combined power and the society wedding would be all anyone would talk about. Romeo and Juliet, minus the part where I kill myself.'

'But you'd kill a part of yourself.' He could see it in her eyes.

She tilted her head. 'It's meant to be a business arrangement. A publicity stunt. We pretend to be a couple, but we live as though we aren't married.'

'What does that mean?'

She shrugged. 'We would have to move to the same house, but other than that, everything would stay the same. I'd have my separate life. He'd have his.'

'He'd have mistresses.'

'So would I. Well, misters.' Her mouth lifted. 'Sounds great, doesn't it?'

'You're not married yet,' he reminded her. 'You're not even engaged. It's not too late.'

She didn't answer him for a long time. It made him wonder if he'd misinterpreted her 'great' as sarcasm. Maybe she *wanted* to marry this Jameson man. Why else would she agree to her father's suggestion?

Had it been a suggestion though? Perhaps it had been a command. But why would she obey it? What was the worst thing that could happen if she didn't?

'Elena,' he said softly. 'What are you not telling me?'

She looked at him, and what he saw there told him not to prod. So he waited. When the waiting spanned minutes, he reached out and took her hand. As the minutes ticked by, he shifted closer. By the time she spoke, they were standing a breath apart.

His heart was thumping, and he was afraid their proximity would mean she could hear it. Or worse, feel it. Either way, she would know how much this was affecting him. How much the fact that she'd taken the last two steps towards him meant to him. They were sharing an intimacy he hadn't shared with anyone else in their conversation. He was drawn to her physically unlike anyone else. He wanted to kiss her. To share *more* with her.

He didn't want her to marry that man.

'He threatened my job,' she said hoarsely. She was staring up at him with big brown eyes that told him as much as her words did. She was scared. 'He didn't say it outright, but he didn't have to. My father… He's powerful.'

Anger pulsed through his body. 'So am I. I'll get you another job.'

'I don't want another job.' She bit her lip. 'I want this job. *My* job that I worked for, for years. The job that brought me here.' Her voice caught. 'It's not fair.'

He slid an arm around her waist, taking great care to be gentle and not give in to the emotion that told him to throw her over his shoulder and run away with her.

'And now there's this stupid engagement party in four days. *Four days*, Micah. I didn't even agree, but my father's invited everyone to it and the media's latched onto the whispers exactly as my father intended.'

'He's trying to strong-arm you into doing this.'

'Yes.' She let out a shaky breath. 'Along with threatening the one thing he knows means the world to me, he's pulling out all the stops to get me to agree.'

'Has he done this before?'

'Not to this extent.'

'That's why you stopped using his money. Why you put distance in your relationship.' She nodded, though he was really confirming more than asking. 'Why did you go to his office that day? You said hope, but for what?'

She rested her hands on his chest. 'If your mother called you and asked you to do something for her, without warning or context, would you do it?'

And finally, he saw. He understood. She'd hoped for a relationship, for the love of a parent. She worried that if she didn't do this, she would lose not only her job, but that chance of love. As someone who'd spent his entire life searching for that love, doing what he thought he had to in order to get that love, he couldn't judge her. It was an impossible situation for a child. His heart broke for her even as he hated her father for putting her in that situation in the first place.

She cracked the first real smile she'd given since they started talking. 'You understand now why I jumped at the chance to be here. To escape it.'

She gently pulled away from him and walked towards the bed.

'Besides, you know, it being a wonderful opportunity. Writing a cover story is career gold for me. Or it was,' she said, narrowing her eyes at him. 'Now that I know I wasn't asked because of my skill, the ask has been tainted.'

He winced. 'I'm sorry. But regardless of how the opportunity came about, you're here, right? You do a good job, it won't matter how you got here.'

She opened her mouth, but no sound came out for a while. 'That's a good point.'

'That hurt, didn't it?'

She smirked. 'Maybe.'

He studied her, but her expression was as closed a book as it had been open earlier. He thought about pushing, but it didn't feel right. So he simply said, 'They wouldn't have agreed for you to write the story if you hadn't earned it, Elena.'

'I believe you. What?' she said in response to his surprise. 'You have pull with a demographic we've been struggling with for some time. Millennials. A solid portion of who will find you attractive. They need this story to be good.'

His face burned. 'We weren't talking about me.'

'No, we weren't.' She smiled. 'It's cute that you're flustered by people finding you attractive.'

'Why couldn't you just take the compliment and leave it at that?' he grumbled.

Her smile widened. 'Thank you for your compliment.' She put a hand on her hip. 'You know, I came here to forget. Not to rehash all of this.' She shook her shoulders. 'I needed an Italian escape with a tycoon, not an Italian confession with one.'

'You're strange, you know that?' Her laugh warmed the parts inside him he hadn't realise had gone cold during her story. 'But you have a point. I can't do much about your decision, but I can distract you. Have you made any plans for Venice yet?'

'Some.' She closed the space between them. 'Nothing that can't be cancelled.'

'I'll work around them.'

Tentatively, he opened his arms. She immediately stepped into them. Rested her head on his chest. It was comfortable. Warm. It felt exactly right.

'We'll make these the best days of your life.'

'Thank you.'

He couldn't resist the kiss he pressed to her forehead in reply.

CHAPTER TEN

WHEN ELENA WOKE the next morning, she asked herself whether she'd dreamed the night before. Micah had apologised and opened up to her about his family. In turn, she had told him about the impossible situation with her father. Now, they were going to spend the remaining days in Italy exploring Venice.

It was wild. But her life had, over the last month, been wild. Unrecognisable. One day she'd been living the life she created for herself, the next day she was contemplating marriage to a stranger. She hadn't paid attention to how little she'd liked the disruption. She had simply been focused on getting through it.

Micah forced her to think about it though. Spending time with him, being attracted to him, talking to him. It made her think about how she didn't like what her father was doing. It made her realise the full capacity of what Cliff was asking her to sacrifice.

It wasn't so much marriage itself, since the institution was easily escapable, as her parents' marriage had shown. If the marriage was based on normal things, that was. Love or respect or mutual admiration. Things that might fade over time. But *her* marriage would be a business contract. Those were harder to get out of. Business contracts with her father would be impossible to get out of. Was a job, however much she loved it, worth sacrificing her freedom for? Was the chance—the *chance*—of her father's love and approval worth giving up her future?

It caused her chest to ache, that thought. The *knowledge*. She knew that her father wouldn't change simply because she'd done what he'd asked. She'd had years and years of experience that told her that wouldn't happen. He would go back to ignoring her—or, worse, using her again and again because she was more accessible to him. It would break her. But now the question was whether giving up the hope of a proper relationship with her father would break her more than that would.

The emptiness and hurt echoing in her body reminded her why she hadn't examined her feelings about the situation. She shut them down, took a shower, and prepared for her day with Micah. He would ensure that she'd forget her problems, at least for the next few days. Her eagerness for him had nothing to do with *him* though. Things might have shifted slightly between them the night before, but this? This was all about forgetting her situation. It had nothing to do with him.

Her heart begged to differ when she got to breakfast. It skipped a beat when Micah looked up from his tablet and smiled. His teeth were white against his brown skin, bouncing off the white of the linen shirt he wore. When he stood, she saw he'd paired the shirt with dark blue chinos and white sneakers that could have been brand new, they were so immaculate.

'You look pretty hip,' she said, taking a seat opposite him.

'I had to look decent since I was spending the day with you.'

She pinched her thigh under the table so she wouldn't swoon at those words. 'What did you look like before?'

'A businessperson.'

'Ah, yes, and we both know businesspeople don't look decent.'

He narrowed his eyes. 'I wanted to look appropriately tourist-like.'

'You absolutely succeed.' She gestured around them. 'As you can see, most of the tourists here look as if they've walked off the catwalk.'

'Elena,' he said, expression pained, 'would you like me to change?'

'I was teasing.' She shook her napkin out and set it on her lap. 'You should have known that, since I was clearly complimenting you. Are you nervous about how you look or something?'

'No.'

He said it too quickly. He *was* nervous, so much so that he didn't want to talk about it. She had questions: Was it because the clothes were new? Did he never dress casually? Had he never simply been a tourist before? Were all his experiences overseas business?

She asked none of it. Because he'd clearly tried, for her benefit, and that was sweeter than she knew how to articulate.

'I think there was a compliment in there for

me, too,' she said instead. 'Clearly you're aspiring to my fashion sense and I appreciate that.'

She wondered if he knew how much relief was in his smile.

'You do look…er…decent today. I like the crown.'

She smiled and touched the arrangement of flowers on her head. 'I bought it in a shop nearby. It's ridiculously extra, but I like it. Plus, it makes me look like a silly tourist and I kind of like that.' She rolled her eyes. 'I know it's silly. Who wants to look like a tourist? It's like putting a target on my back. Or on my forehead. But I don't know, I guess…'

She trailed off at the way he was looking at her. 'What?'

'You're rambling.'

'Micah,' she said slowly, 'I know you're not an expert on social interactions, but pointing things like that out isn't polite.'

'I thought you wanted me to be honest?'

She had nothing to say to that. Because yeah, she wanted him to be honest. But how did she tell him there was a thing like being too honest?

His chuckle drew her out of her confusion. 'Oh, you think this is funny?'

'It is.' He grinned. 'Payback is always fun.'

'Payback... Oh, for your clothes?' At his nod, she laughed. 'Haven't you heard the phrase "Revenge is a dish best served cold"?'

'I've never been a big believer of that. Personally, I think revenge is best served as soon as possible so neither party forgets.'

'Your brain is a wonder,' she said, shaking her head.

'Thank you.'

She rolled her eyes at that response. 'So. What's on the agenda today?'

She stole his coffee as he went through their day, interrupting occasionally to ask a question or tease him. He made it so easy. He often said something that could be understood in several different ways, and she would purposely understand the wrong meanings. That frustrated him, or annoyed him, which made her laugh, then he would laugh, and it all made her breathe more easily than she had in a long time.

It was leaps and bounds away from how she'd perceived him before. He was still charming, but that charm came from him being himself. From his mistakes, his laughter. The way he wasn't performing a persona. She didn't think he'd appreciate if she announced it to the world, but he didn't mind being that way with her. She felt touched. And warm. That warmth was so precious that she held it close, like the only light in a room of darkness.

That metaphor was alarming, even to her.

'I know that I shouldn't be this excited to go on a boat since I've done it before, but this makes me so happy.'

Elena did a little stomp with her legs, before twirling in a circle. It made the skirt of her dress whirl around her. Micah tried to focus on the top half of her, but there was a delay in the shift of his gaze—he couldn't help it— and he got a glimpse of full brown flesh. It was as enticing as the rest of her. She wore a bright yellow dress, as if she'd realised how much sunlight she'd brought to his life. With her flower crown, she looked like a summer goddess.

It worried him how badly he wanted to worship her.

'It isn't a boat. It's a gondola.'

'My mistake,' she said blandly, and made him smile. She did that a lot. And he was smiling more than he ever had before. That worried him, too. But it didn't stop him from smiling at her. Or from thinking about how different she was now, when she wasn't thinking about the decision she had to make.

What if she didn't have to make it?

He couldn't pay attention to the thought when the gondolier called for them to get in. He did, using the man's help, then gently nudged him aside to help Elena. She smiled brightly, and it became obvious why he'd wanted to help her. Apparently, he would do anything to get that smile. To keep it there, too.

It stuck as they sat down and the gondola began to float down the canal. It was a bright, sunny day, and the blue-green of the water around them sparkled as it stretched between buildings. A gentleman began to sing, rich and deep, and Elena sighed at his side. She snuggled closer, not intentionally, he didn't think, but it made him hold his breath.

That might not have been the right description of it. It was more like someone was squeezing his lungs, so he had less capacity to breathe. He'd felt that way the entire day. When they'd been exploring the stores around St Mark's Square. Or when Elena had insisted on feeding the pigeons, then got alarmed when more and more of them came.

'What is it with you and pigeons?' he'd asked. 'I told you this wouldn't end well.'

'I thought you were exaggerating. You exaggerate.'

'You live in Cape Town, Elena. You've been to the Waterfront. You know what pigeons are like.'

'I thought European pigeons would be different.'

He'd laughed, harder when she hid behind him. She'd ended up giving the bag of seeds to a kid before running away, causing the pigeons to scatter. They'd eaten pasta and chocolate crêpes and taken pictures. Once, Elena had photobombed another couple, then apologised profusely and taken about twenty pictures of them alone to make up for it. Now they were here, on the canal, having someone sing to them.

It was a lot to process. Not the experience,

but the emotions that accompanied it. And the thoughts. Those insidious thoughts that had popped into his mind all day, then scurried away before he could put his finger on what they were suggesting. They all pooled together now though, growing into an idea that stole his breath.

It was based on never wanting to see Elena as tortured as she had been the night before. To keep her as happy as she was now, as she had been all day. It was built by the memories of how she'd elevated his business banquet that night in Rome because she fitted so perfectly into his world. She went head to head with him when he did something stupid, forced him to think about the way he treated people, and made him feel more like himself than he ever had. If he'd ever encountered his equal, she was it.

She was it.

'This is so nice,' Elena said at that moment, as if sensing his confusing thoughts. And his body, as if confused itself, responding by putting an arm around Elena's shoulders.

He froze. Until she rested her entire body against him. Then he melted.

It was like the hug from the night before. Warm and comfortable. Except there was more now. She was looking up at him, smiling, and he felt himself stumble. Whatever part of him had been standing steady in the face of the onslaught that Elena was unknowingly waging against him broke down. Whatever sanity he had left that told him not to indulge his ridiculous idea fled.

The proposal spilled out of his mouth.

'Marry me.'

CHAPTER ELEVEN

ELENA DIDN'T HAVE a moment to process before the clouds of celebration broke above her and it began to rain.

'A proposal!' the gondolier cried. He shouted in Italian to another gondolier close by. 'A proposal!' he said again.

'Oh, no,' Elena started to say, shaking her head, but the man had stopped steering.

He reached out to take Micah's hand, then grabbed both of Elena's and kissed them. When he saw she had no ring, he clapped, shouting about spontaneity and romance in Italian to his colleagues. There were two women who squealed happily, and another who wished them well quietly. All the while, Elena couldn't say a word. Micah replied to them weakly, accepting the congratulations as more gondolas drew near.

By the time they reached land again, Elena had regained her composure. She smiled her thanks and waved at the women who'd squealed earlier. She let Micah help her out of the boat and even managed a smile for him. Their gondolier was still looking at them with pride, and she allowed him to hug her.

When they were walking away from all the commotion, Elena felt herself deflate. She almost stumbled down a set of stairs, but a steady arm snaked around her waist. It seared through her clothing, and, despite the drama he'd caused in the last hour, reminded her they had something.

But that didn't mean she wanted to marry him. She was still working through the situation with her father and Jameson. How was she supposed to marry Micah with that going on? And what had provoked his proposal in the first place? They had spent a lovely day together, yes, but a day didn't make a marriage.

Or was it the *more* that could make their marriage? She'd felt connected to him from the moment they'd met, after all. She'd been comparing her relationship with Jameson to him ever since then. Oh, no. This…this *thing* he'd done was making her lose her mind. She didn't appreciate it. Not one bit.

Micah had the wisdom not to try to talk to her until they were back at the hotel. Wordlessly, he followed her to her room. She stepped back to allow him inside, then closed the door and leaned her back against it. Neither of them spoke for a long while.

'What just happened?' she asked eventually.

'I… I proposed.'

He looked as stunned as she felt.

'Yes, you did. I suppose that question was too vague, then. *Why* did you propose?'

'I don't know.' He looked at her. Ran a hand over his head. 'No—I do know.'

She waited for the rest.

He sighed. 'I wanted to save you from marrying someone you didn't know.'

He seemed genuine. And his motives were… she didn't want to say pure, because that had implications she didn't want to think about. He was well intentioned.

Still.

'You can't just propose to someone, Micah.'

'I know.'

'I mean, it's one thing if we were dating and this was a surprise. In which case, a proposal on a gondola would be appropriate.' Perfect, actually. Because if she removed the fact that he'd put her on the spot, and that they weren't dating, she would have been thrilled with the proposal. 'But obviously this isn't a romantic proposal. It's a business proposal.'

He didn't answer for a beat. 'It's another option. From a…' he hesitated '…a friend.'

Friends. That description didn't seem right to her. It seemed inadequate. But at the same time, she'd rather he call her a friend than try to figure out what other label fit.

'I don't know what to say, Micah. We've only known one another for days. We spent a solid portion of that time not speaking.'

'But when we spoke, it meant something, didn't it?' he asked quietly. 'And days might not be long, but it's longer than what you've spent with the man your father wants you to marry. Isn't it?' he prodded when she didn't reply.

She nodded. Not only to his question, but to the rest of what he said. She knew him better than she knew Jameson. She trusted him more than she trusted Jameson. Which wasn't saying much, considering how little she trusted Jameson. Relief rippled through her.

She quickly realised it was because the notion of trusting Micah…was nerve-racking. Thinking that she didn't trust him *that much* felt safer than thinking that she did. After what he'd done to her, the games he'd played, she was right to be cautious.

But he'd also apologised for doing that. He'd had a sincere motive, which she, of all people, could understand. He'd tried to earn back her trust. Told her the truth about his parents and cancelled all his plans to spend the last few days in Italy with her. She felt comforted in his arms; she felt alive in his arms.

But did that mean he was a safer choice than marrying Jameson?

'Why marry you?' she asked, a little desperately. 'Shouldn't I just say no to my father?'

He walked over to her refrigerator and took another bottle of water. He downed it as quickly as he had the bottle the day before.

'According to my understanding, if you say no to your father, you'll be punished,' he said long after he finished drinking. 'You'll lose a job that's important to you. I assume that puts you in a difficult position with your financial responsibilities. And you obviously won't be offered help from your father. Not that you'd accept it.'

She angled her head, accepting all his pre-suppositions.

'I can keep you from losing your job.'

She blinked. 'How?'

He gave her a wry smile. 'The same way I got you to do this story on me.'

'You can…you can really do that?'

'I can.'

'No,' she said, shaking her head. 'My father is powerful. He has connections. Friends. He'll buy the paper if he has to.'

'I'll buy the company that owns the paper,' Micah said patiently. 'I can arrange for it before we go home.'

'Wh—why?'

'If you're my wife, I'll do anything I have to in order to protect you.'

And he had the power to, she realised. He could fight her father on his level. He could *beat* him. She would never have to do anything her father bid her to do again if she had Micah protecting her.

It removed the fear of her losing her job and security from the equation of the Jameson situation. But what about the rest? She paced the floor, silently thanking Micah for giving her a moment to think. The media would go wild for a marriage between her and Micah. She was an heiress; he was a self-made millionaire. And they got married after she was assigned to write a story about him? It was a romance novel in real life, and the press would portray it as such. The focus from the tragedy at the John diamond mine would shift, and the John image would be elevated.

Her father would love it.

As for the business… Her father would love that, too, if she was honest. He would love to hitch his wagon to Micah's star. Micah was a fresh, young businessperson who would invigorate John Diamond Company's image—and potentially the business itself—and make Cliff John look like a visionary.

Had Micah thought about that, too?

'What's in this for you?'

'Beyond helping a friend?' She narrowed her eyes. He smiled. 'Fine. I can't deny the business advantages our partnership will have.'

'You mean a partnership with my father.'

No, I mean *our* partnership. You were magnificent at the banquet, Elena. Your presence there is part of the reason Lucca and the rest of the Vittoria board are looking forward to working with me.'

'You could have achieved that without me.'

'I would have mangled my speech, annoyed people with my bluntness, and had them whispering about me learning humility if it wasn't for you.' The ends of his mouth tilted up. 'You make me look good. You make my business look good. Advantages.'

Stunned, she swallowed. 'This has…nothing to do with my father?'

'I've been planning to pitch to him for years,' he said, smile disappearing. 'That won't change if we marry. It can't.' His eyes pleaded with her to understand.

She did. Even if it stung a little.

'Of course.'

'I can make sure whatever business we do together doesn't affect you in any way.' He moved closer to her, but didn't touch her. 'I can protect you from him.'

'Can you stop me from wanting his love, too? No,' she said quickly. 'That was unfair.

I'm sorry.' Her legs were shaking, so she sat down on the bed. 'This is a lot to think about.'

He came to sit next to her. 'I know. And I'll give you as long as you need. As long as is feasible, considering your father wants to announce your engagement to another man in a matter of days.'

She nodded, but didn't speak.

'I'll give you every assurance you need to feel safe,' he said softly. 'Not in the form of promises, but in a contract. We can stipulate everything legally. If I do anything to break that contract, you can take me to the cleaners.'

Her lips curved. 'I don't want your money.'

'I know. It's part of the reason I want to marry you.'

'Worried about gold-diggers?'

He gave a surprised laugh. 'No. I was thinking that your reasons for marrying me are nobler than money.' He paused. 'But come to think of it, it would be nice not to worry about gold-diggers.'

She snorted, but her mind was already wandering. Past all the business stuff, past her father, both of which they agreed on. It settled on the more dangerous things. The emotions that sat in a tight little ball in her chest marked with Micah's name. If that ball ever unfurled, it would cause untold damage. It was more likely to unfurl if they were married. As would the physical attraction she had for him. That ball sat *much* lower, felt like fire whenever he touched her, and begged her to touch him.

'You joke now,' she said, desperate to get away from the thoughts that made her heart pound, 'but what if you want a real relationship one day? What if you fall in love with someone and—what?' she asked at his smile.

'I barely managed to keep this friendship alive, Elena. I have no hopes that I'll be able to keep a flirtation alive, let alone a real relationship.'

'If you speak with them the way you've spoken with me—'

'Let me rephrase,' he interrupted. 'I don't want to flirt, or date, or marry. For real, I mean.' His smile was wry now. 'It's too much time and effort. I won't be missing out on anything by marrying you. But if you feel like you will be—'

'I don't.' She sighed. 'I just want to focus on

work and—' She stopped herself. 'Children. What about children?'

He frowned. 'Never thought about them.'

'But do you want them?' she pressed.

'Do you?' he countered.

She shook her head vehemently. 'If I have my parents' genes in me, it would be better for both me and the non-existent child if we didn't cross paths.'

'You would be a great mother.'

'We'll never find out,' she told him.

'Agreed.'

'So easily?'

'I've never thought about them, and you don't want them. Seems pretty easy to me.'

She studied him. 'You're being pretty cool about this. Too cool, for someone who's about to be married.'

'You haven't said yes yet.'

She almost said it then, but thought better of it.

'I need time to think.'

To figure out if saving myself from this situation I'm in with Jameson is worth risking you hurting me some day.

'You have as long as you need.' He stood. 'Just remember this.'

She looked at him. 'What?'

'There could be worse things than being married to someone who respects you. Who you respect. Hopefully,' he added.

'I do,' she said softly. And knew he was right.

Micah called his lawyers immediately after he left Elena's room. He paid them a lot of money for the privilege of their advice, though he did feel bad about the hour. Not bad enough not to call them. He wanted to be ready if Elena agreed to his proposal. And he had a feeling she would. Which meant he might be married soon.

He should have been worried. Anxious. Something along those lines. He shouldn't be feeling...whatever he was feeling now. A hum, a buzz inside him. As if he'd consumed a swarm of bees and they were making their way through his body. He wouldn't call the feeling excitement. More anticipation.

He couldn't deny the advantages to marrying Elena. Everything he told her was true.

She was the perfect business spouse; her linguistic skills were more helpful than he could have imagined; it would make a potential business partnership with her father easier. But he hadn't only been thinking about business when he proposed. He'd been caught by her. In the way the sun glinted off her hair. The smell of the salt of the canal and the perfume on her skin. When she was tucked into his side, he felt fortified. He felt whole. An illusion, he knew. No one could make him whole besides himself.

But that was it. Elena made him feel as though he *could* make himself whole. He hadn't even known the version of himself when he was with her existed, to be frank. He laughed, relaxed. His brain turned off, not constantly calculating or devising his next steps. It was different from how he'd been in the thirty-two years of his life and he liked it. He liked who he was with her.

And *that* should have worried him. That there was more than business involved in his decision to propose. That he was considering marriage at all when it hadn't appealed to him in the past. His parents hadn't married, so he didn't have anything to—or not to—emulate. And the people around him who were married treated the institution cavalierly. Adultery and disrespect were as much a part of marriage for his peers as their spouses were. Micah had no doubts, considering what his research revealed about the man, that Elena's would-be fiancé would follow that custom if they did marry.

It highlighted another alarming reason for his proposal: he wanted to protect her. From her father, who seemed callous and uncaring of the woman Elena was. From the man her father wanted her to marry, who would likely find ways to erase Elena's personality. He couldn't bear the thought of it. She was too vibrant, too vital.

Marriage might not have appealed to him, but being in Elena's presence did. Being in a partnership where they could treat one another as equals and respect each other for who they were? He could get on board with marriage for that.

Why did he just become aware of a slight trepidation kicking with every beat of his heart?

He went to the bar and took out a tiny bottle of brandy. He poured half of it into a glass and drank it, then poured the other half into it and added ice. He took the glass to the sliding doors, and opened them to Venice.

Laughter and music from some far-off place drifted up to him. He couldn't see much, but he could hear the water of the canal. It lapped against buildings, lightly, so that the sound was barely more than a whisper. The light breeze was likely the cause of it, but as it touched his face Micah couldn't fault it. The balcony he stood on was small, about five steps away from his hotel room, but it was enough to house two small chairs. He settled into one, and tried to figure out that trepidation.

Downsides. There had to be a downside to marrying Elena. *Everything* had downsides. There would be legal complications that came with being married, wouldn't there? But he had a team of competent lawyers and both he and Elena would stipulate the terms of the agreement. That didn't seem so much of a downside as it was admin. He could handle admin.

Children. He had never thought about them. To him, that said enough. Children deserved parents who wanted them. At the very least, parents who thought about wanting them. He had no desire to repeat the mistakes of his parents. Elena didn't want children either. That solved the problem easily, if making prospects for the physical part of their relationship less exciting.

Well. That posed a problem he didn't think could be easily solved. He couldn't see himself dating if he was married to Elena. Not only because the thought made him slightly nauseous for reasons he'd rather not examine, but because no woman had appealed to him the way Elena did. He had no interest in discovering if someone in the future could appeal to him in that way. It complicated sating his physical needs. But could the same be said for Elena?

If she wanted to go outside their marriage, he would have to respect it. He didn't own her; he didn't believe marriage or any relationship would change that. But he didn't want her to go outside their marriage. He wanted her to turn to him if she needed…that.

And *that* was a downside that made things a hell of a lot harder for the both of them.

CHAPTER TWELVE

'DO YOU UNPACK your belongings when you're staying at a hotel, or do you keep things in your luggage?'

Elena thought it was a strange morning greeting from a man who had just proposed to her, but she answered. 'I keep most things in my luggage. Generally my toiletries go in the bathroom and I have to pack those up. Good morning, by the way.' She slid into the booth opposite Micah. 'Did you sleep well?'

'I had a solid three hours, yeah.'

'Three hours?' She lifted her brows. 'Did you have something to think about?'

He smiled. It was teasing and a little sly, and it made her stomach jump. Or was that her hunger? In the whirlwind of the night before, she hadn't eaten. She'd drunk numerous cups of tea as she'd sat up and thought Micah's proposal through. She'd exhausted herself, but she thought she had an answer. That smile was making her doubt it though. Could she be his wife if his smile made her—?

Hungry, she interrupted her thoughts. She was *hungry*.

I bet.

It was as if her thoughts were punishing her for interrupting them.

No, she told them firmly. *Stop misbehaving.*

'Yes, I did, which you know.' He eyed her. 'How much sleep did you get?'

She pretended to count. 'Oh, about three hours, too. They weren't solid though.'

'I'm sorry.'

She waved away the apology. 'You weren't in bed keeping me awake. Oh, you ordered me coffee?' she exclaimed when the waiter put a cup down in front of her. 'You're a lifesaver.'

He didn't reply, but his eyes had gone intense again. Not that it said much; that was his normal state. Although he had seemed lighter recently. Lighter compared to who he usually was, which was saying something, what with the proposal.

'What's wrong?' she asked when she'd taken a drink of her coffee and he was still staring at her.

'Nothing. You said… Never mind.' He picked up his menu. 'I'm thinking full breakfast this morning. It's going to be a long day.'

'Hold on. I'm still…'

She trailed off, replaying her words. When they caught up with her, she nearly dropped the cup she was bringing to her lips again. Not at what she'd said—that was perfectly harmless if Micah didn't have such a dirty mind—but at his reaction. It told her they needed to talk about that *thing* she'd thought about at several points of the night.

'Why…er…why is today going to be a long day?' she said, drinking her coffee as she intended to. It had nothing to do with the much needed caffeine and everything to do with hiding her blush. It also distracted her from having to talk about sex with her future husband and she was looking forward to that.

Not looking forward to that. *Not.*

In response to that correction, her mind offered her the memory of Micah pinning her to the wall. Heat flooded her body and, instinctively, she pressed her legs together. Then she cursed both her body and her mind for betraying her, and tried not to think about how sensitive every part of her body had suddenly become.

She took another gulp of coffee.

'I…er… I thought we could go to Tuscany.' Micah took a sip from his coffee, too. Were his motives the same as hers? 'There's a small town there that would be perfect for today.'

'Oh, I don't want you to go out of your way to show me Italy. Venice is plenty.'

'But we've done Venice,' he said with a small smile. 'You've seen most of it. Of course, we can spend more time finding the jewels of the city. But wouldn't you rather go to the countryside? Sip wine in the vineyards? Eat homemade pasta?'

She stared at him for a long time. 'You're a hell of a businessperson. I'm pretty stubborn, but I swear you can talk me into almost anything.'

'Almost anything?' he enquired gently.

She opened her mouth to tell him what she'd decided, but the words wouldn't come out. She frowned. Was she being cautious? Or did she feel hesitant?

'It's okay, Elena.' His eyes were softer than usual. 'We don't have to talk about it now.'

'But we have to talk about it,' she insisted.

'We will. After the wine and pasta.' He smiled.

'You already know me so well,' she teased, though a part of her meant it. 'But yes, wine and pasta it is.'

That was how Elena found herself in the beautiful town of San Gimignano later that morning. It took them some time to get there by train, but the journey was beautiful. Green stretched out through the windows for kilometres as Micah told her about San Gimignano as if he were a tour guide. That was how she knew that the town was in the heart of Italy's wine country, and that it had narrow streets and old architecture much like Italy's cities.

But his descriptions couldn't prepare her for the feeling she got once they were there. It felt like history and peace, an uncommon combination, yet somehow it captured the atmosphere perfectly. The buildings were tall and old, as promised, but they felt rich with culture and were beautiful. They stretched up like stone trees to the sky, with ivy creeping up them as if wanting to see the sky, too.

They stopped at a rustic restaurant Micah

had been to before, and were guided to a terrace that overlooked the vineyards. The terrace itself was beautiful. Flowers were planted in a large square in the middle of the space, and terracotta pots with flowers stood on the boundaries of it.

They were seated at the edge of the terrace and had the best view. Then the wine and the pasta came, and Elena thought it was the best day.

'Are you trying to persuade me to marry you, Micah?' she teased when their meal was done. She wouldn't have done it, but it was her third glass of the delicious wine, and she was in a teasing mood.

'You'll have to tell me if it's working before I admit that,' he said with a small smile. He was as tipsy as her, unless he could hold his wine better than she could. She doubted that.

'It might be.' She sighed contently. 'I've been more relaxed yesterday and today than I've ever been in my life.' She thought about it. 'In fact, this entire trip has done a world of good for my mental health. Despite those unexpectedly tense moments between us.'

'Tense moments?'

'Oops. Probably shouldn't have said that. But don't pretend like you don't know what I'm talking about.' She wagged a finger at him, then used the hand to count down the tense incidents. 'In the plane, when you looked at me in my unicorn shirt. At the banquet when you pinned me against the wall. After the banquet when we fought about—' she waved her hand '—something. Our conversation in my hotel room. The proposal.' She waved her hand at him. 'We need to stop it now or I'll run out of fingers to count on.'

'You have another hand.'

'Good point. Though that's not *my* point, so maybe it isn't.'

'Are you drunk, Elena?' he asked, this time with his annoyingly sexy smile on display.

'Of course I'm not drunk.' She said it a tad loud. She knew that because the people at the table next to her looked over in amusement. 'Hmm. Maybe I should switch to water.'

She studied her wine glass, drank the last drop then filled it with water and downed that.

'At least it has the same taste as the wine.'

'You're cute when you're drunk.'

She snorted. 'Please. We both know I'm cute when I'm sober, too.'

His smile went from his lips to his eyes. Somehow. He wasn't smiling at her, but she could tell he was still amused, and it had something to do with his eyes. Hmm. He could definitely hold his wine better than she could. She would have to remember that for their marriage.

Their marriage. She was marrying him. And she hadn't told him yet. She should probably tell him.

'We need to talk about sex,' she said instead.

And the shock of it sobered her right up.

'Do you want some dessert?' the server asked, oblivious to the tension between him and Elena.

'No,' he said quickly.

'But coffee, please,' Elena added.

'And for you, sir?'

'No. Yes. Yes,' he repeated. He could do with some coffee if they were going to be having this conversation.

The server disappeared, but Elena didn't say anything. She poured herself another glass of water and drank it, though slower than she had before. He suspected it was to delay the conversation, but he would wait as long as he had to. It was a skill he'd mastered in business negotiations, waiting. There was no way he would speak before she did. Let alone on this topic.

'I'm sorry,' she said, clearing her throat. 'I shouldn't have been so blunt about it.'

Micah drank from his water glass, too. He didn't want her to think he was panicked at her bringing this up. In fact, he was elated. It meant they were on the same page in terms of what they were trying to prepare for with their marriage. It meant she was probably thinking about saying yes to him. It meant he wouldn't have to bring it up.

'It's fine. You want to talk about it, we can talk about it.'

'Are we calling it "it" like we're two teenagers?' she asked lightly. '"Are we going to do 'it', Micah?"' She was shaking her head before she even finished. 'I am so sorry I did that. The fact that it went through my filter tells me I should have stopped after that second glass.'

'Elena, it's okay. You're just nervous.' He couldn't help his chuckle though.

She gave him an unimpressed look. 'If I was—and I'm not saying I am—the only thing I'd want from you is your laughter. So, thank you.'

He lifted up his hands, and shut his mouth. But she was so adorable. Her cheeks were red from the wine or the sun, he didn't know. Both, he decided. Her hair was an intricate web of curls at the top of her head, slightly off balance because of the hat she'd replaced the flower crown with. She'd brightened as soon as she'd put it on, and walked around with it all day until now, despite the bulk it created on her head.

She was wearing another charming summer dress, white and red this time, and had paired it with her signature red lipstick. It was faded from the food she'd eaten and wine she'd drunk, but he could still see. He wanted to kiss her lips.

'Okay, before I get there, I need to say that I'm... I'm going to say yes to marrying you.'

Her words didn't have the lyrical cadence they'd had earlier, and he thought the water was working fast. Then he realised she'd told him what he wanted and he wasn't process-ing it. The server arrived before he could and, after he thanked the man, Elena began to speak again.

'I need to talk to you about two things first though. One is sex, but we'll get to that. Not to the sex. To the topic.' She frowned and stared at the black coffee. 'I should have ordered an espresso.'

He didn't speak, half amused, half entranced by her words. By everything about her.

'Look, you've never had a personal…friend-ship, or whatever, like this before. I don't mean physically—' she blushed, but pressed on '—but emotionally. You've never had some-one who wants to spend time with you. Not the business you, or millionaire you or what-ever you, but *you*. I…um…care about you, and I guess you sense that, and I just wanted you to know that you don't have to marry me be-cause I'm the first person to do that.'

She bit her lip at the end of it, as if keeping herself from adding to what she said. What more could she add? He almost asked her, but now he was thinking about whether she was right. Was he offering to marry her because he felt obligated to? Was this a response to someone who cared about him?

He had no means of comparison, so he struggled to answer that question. He didn't know what a personal friendship—or whatever, he thought wryly—was like. His relationship with his parents was non-existent, so he wasn't sure how he responded to love. Which sounded dramatic since he knew his parents loved him. In their way. So if he was responding to love, it was to his brand of love. The fact that someone loved him in a way that he could actually feel.

Wait—not love, care. Elena cared about him. He was responding to how she *cared* about him.

'How would I know if I'm doing that?'

Elena tilted her head. 'I'm not sure.'

'How do you know you're not accepting me because you don't know what any of that looks like either?'

Her lips parted, then formed an oh. She gave a little laugh. 'I guess I don't know that either.'

He brought his coffee to his lips. 'It's not

exactly something I hoped you and I would have in common.'

'We have plenty of other things in common,' she said with a shake of her head. She continued, but he made a mental note to ask about those things later. 'And I came up with an answer. Kind of.' The knit in her brow deepened. 'We know how we felt when our parents treated us the way they did.' She paused. 'The not great stuff, and the way it made us feel. I don't feel that way now, with you.' She swallowed. 'But there was one time my father...almost acted proud of me.' She looked down, as if she were ashamed. He barely stopped himself from reaching out to her. 'And it made me feel...warm. Valued.' Now she met his eyes. 'Kind of how you make me feel.'

He had no idea what to do with the feelings that admission awoke in him. It felt as if a volcano had burst. He tried to focus on something else; *anything* other than the hot lava of emotion spreading inside him. Logic chose her relationship with her father. What she told him helped him understand why she was so eager to please the man. She wanted to feel warm and valued again. He couldn't blame her for that. Especially not when he wanted to feel that way just once with his parents.

Especially not when she made him feel that way, too.

Something skittish skipped through his chest.

'I'm sorry. I didn't mean to make things so sombre.'

'You didn't.'

Her eyes softened. 'I appreciate that lie.'

'Elena,' he said slowly, trying to get his thoughts in order. 'There are many reasons I asked you to marry me. Many logical reasons that have nothing to do with the fact that you…care about me.'

'Oh. Yes, of course.' She gave a quick shake of her head. 'I didn't mean to imply—'

'But,' he interrupted, 'the fact that you're concerned I might be doing this for less straightforward reasons, if you will, is also a part of why I asked. You're a rare breed of person,' he continued carefully. 'I would be honoured to be your husband.'

Their eyes met, held, and he was reminded of the lava again.

Which he promptly fell into when she said, 'Even at the cost of what you want to achieve with your mother?'

CHAPTER THIRTEEN

'WHAT DO YOU MEAN?' Micah asked once he resurfaced.

'What if my father chooses to punish me for going against his wishes by refusing to partner with you?' Her voice was low. 'You said that plan had something to do with your mother, didn't you?'

'Yes,' he murmured, realising he hadn't told her the details of it. 'She cares about her career more than anything else. I thought she would care about mine, too, if I partnered with your father. He's her biggest client.'

'And if she cared about your career, she might start to care more about you, too.'

He gave a curt nod. She studied him for a while.

'Is it worth it, Micah? Am I...? Is *this* worth the risk?'

It was a damn good question. And the fact that she was asking it meant more to him than he could comprehend. It told him it was worth the risk. Despite her deliberate rephrasing, he thought *she* was worth the risk. His gut agreed. It also told him she would care about him even if he didn't do anything to make her care about him.

She wasn't like his mother.

It was a confusing realisation in the context of everything that was happening. His mother was the reason he and Elena were even having this conversation. His desire to get her attention had put him on this path. Now he was considering throwing that away? Why? Because someone was offering him a relationship he didn't have to work so damn hard for?

Yes.

The lack of turmoil he felt at that was refreshing.

'I don't know what it means that I'm saying this.' He spoke slowly, in case something changed. It didn't. 'But I'd still like to marry you.'

'Micah,' Elena breathed. She reached out and covered his hand with hers. 'Are you sure?'

He turned his hand over and threaded his fingers through hers. 'Yes.'

Elena studied him. Seconds later, she shifted to the seat beside him, then grabbed his hand again.

'There's no shame in wanting a relationship with your mother. Even at the cost of this.'

'I know.' Because he couldn't resist it, he cupped her face. 'But I think my life will be fuller with you in it. My life will just be... different, with my mother in it.'

Emotion flooded her eyes. 'I'm sorry,' she whispered, clasping her hands around the wrist of the hand that held her face.

He could tell she meant it. She wasn't controlling her facial expressions. She was showing him her heart and, in it, he could see her sincerity. And more. So much more. More than he'd ever thought he could hope for when anyone looked at him.

'You don't have to be sorry for something outside your control,' he said.

'Not marrying you is *inside* my control.'

'It wouldn't make a difference to my relationship with my mother.' Somehow he knew that with certainty. 'I have no guarantee working with your father would either. I do know that marrying you would make a difference to my life.'

She bit her lip, her eyes not leaving his. 'Are you sure?'

He nodded. 'If you are.'

She nodded, too. 'I am.'

'Then let's get married.'

'We need to talk about something else first.'

He dropped his hand and groaned. 'I think we've talked enough.'

'You're right.' Her eyes sparkled. 'Maybe we should try a kiss, then?'

She didn't care that she was being forward. Micah's actual proposal had been clumsy—romantic, but clumsy—but this? This admission of what he thought his life would be with her in it? It was swoon-worthy. It was movie-worthy. It was romance-novel-worthy, kiss-you-until-you're-breathless-worthy. She wanted to be breathless.

'Are you sure?' he asked, though he'd already shifted forward, bringing their lips close together.

'I wouldn't have suggested it if I weren't.'

'Ah, yes. I forget you say what you mean.'

He put his hand at the base of her neck. It sent a shiver through her. 'It's refreshing.'

'So you keep saying.'

Now she moved closer, running her index finger around the button at the top of his shirt. It was another white shirt, like the day before, except this one was short sleeved instead of rolled up. It revealed round biceps, and, before she'd fully thought it through, she was running her finger along the veins she could see there.

'You know what *would* be refreshing?' she said lazily. 'If you stopped talking and kissed me.'

She only had a flash of his smile before his lips met hers.

The sensation was other-worldly. A foolish description. A fanciful description. It fit. Not once in her lifetime on earth had she felt so consumed by a kiss as she did now. The world around them ceased to exist. Only the heat that went from her lips down to her core, trailing a path that pulsed with desire, existed.

Then he slipped his tongue into her mouth, and she realised that existed, too.

It was probably a good idea to establish that both their bodies existed on this plane she was on. Her hands had somehow found both his biceps, and were holding on for dear life. His hands were resting on her thighs, squeezing her flesh as if anchoring his fingers there. Their mouths moved in union, giving and taking, enjoying and lusting.

There was more to the lusting than the physical. It felt deeper. It felt as if it touched her heart. It raced as Micah kissed her; a testament to his skill and his words. He kissed as intensely as she'd imagined he would, but with a hesitance that told her he was paying attention. To her responses, to her body. To what gave her pleasure so that he could continue to give it.

All of it told her he was a good man. And that, really, was what her heart was reacting to. He made sure she wanted to kiss him before acting on her suggestion. Even now, he was being careful. If his hands ever moved from her thighs, it would be after a question. Either verbally, or through a subtle touch that asked for permission. When she gave it, he would pay attention to her body as thoroughly as he was currently doing to her mouth. He would ask her for guidance, she knew, and would obey when she offered it to him.

He would torture her in all the right ways. His kiss—this simple kiss—told her so. Now, more than ever, she was glad she'd broached the topic of sex with Micah. The sooner they clarified their positions on it, the sooner they could act on those positions. She was certain of what he wanted. She knew what she wanted, too. She had never been as eager to sate her needs with anyone else.

'Micah,' she said, the shock of it forcing her to pull away.

Her breath took a long time to catch up to that shock. As it did, she lifted trembling hands to her mouth. It felt swollen. It felt used. Both felt like triumphs.

'It was too much too soon,' Micah said hoarsely. He reached for his water and emptied the glass in seconds. Then, seemingly having a handle on himself, he poured another glass and handed it to her.

'No, that's not it,' she said, accepting the water.

'Then what?'

Or maybe that *was* it. Not the kiss, but the

realisations. The emotions. Too many too soon. But she couldn't tell him that.

'I was just thinking… I'm glad it's you. Not Jameson, I mean.' She tucked a stray curl behind her ear. 'We wouldn't share that.'

'Did you…er…?' He cleared his throat. 'Did you try?'

She gave him an amused look. 'Did I try to kiss a man who saw me as only a business arrangement? No.'

'Good.'

'Is it?' she asked casually. Colour touched his cheeks. It was the first time she'd ever seen him blush. He shifted, telling her he didn't like it as much as she did, and she took mercy on him. 'Honestly, I don't think Jameson would have ever been interested in me. I don't think I'm his type. Too mouthy.'

She'd been joking, but he didn't crack a smile. He didn't even reply. It wouldn't have been a conversation if he didn't shift, avoiding her gaze.

'What?'

'Nothing,' he said quickly. Too quickly.

'Then why are you acting so weird?'

'No reason.'

'Micah.'

'It's not relevant any more.'

'So you should have no problem telling me then.'

He narrowed his eyes. 'You're just as formidable as you say I am, you know that?'

'Thank you,' she said. 'Now spill.'

After a long pause, he answered. 'I had Serena send me over some information about the man you were going to marry.'

'Did you?' she asked lightly. 'Any particular reason?'

'I was…interested.'

'Hmm.'

'In any case,' he said quickly, 'there was a story from this week that… Well, I'm sure you've seen it. You're a journalist.'

'I don't see *every* story.'

'No, I suppose not.' He cleared his throat. 'You probably have an alert for the man you're thinking about marrying though.'

'Surprisingly, no. But,' she said conversationally, 'if you keep stalling, I might reconsider marrying you. Or spill this glass of water on your pants and tell everyone you've had an accident. Probably the latter. Less dramatic.'

Micah frowned. 'Those are both dramatic options.'

'Micah.'

'Fine.' He cleared his throat for the millionth time. 'There was a photo on a gossip site. It was purely speculation, in light of, I think, the news of your impending engagement. They claimed the man was Jameson St Clair.' He paused. 'With another woman.'

Elena took a second. 'Do you have the link to the story?'

He studied her, but took his phone out, typed on it for a moment, then handed it to her. The headline was salacious, which she expected, but she focused on the picture. It showed a man walking into a hotel with a woman. She was dressed in a sophisticated black dress that was tight and ended above her knee. The man wore a distinctive suit—bright blue, with white pinstripes. It was what Jameson had worn the day her father had suggested their marriage. The shock of the suggestion had every detail embedded in her mind.

Jameson had been with another woman the same day he said he would marry her.

'Well. I guess mouthy has nothing to do with

it. It's because I'm brunette,' she said, handing the phone back to Micah.

'It's him?'

'It is. And that's the same day he and my father said they wanted us to marry. The suit,' she answered when his brows rose. 'It stuck in my mind.'

'I'm sorry.'

'Don't be.' She shrugged. 'This would have been the reality of my life. You've given me another option.' She reached for the coffee they'd both forgotten, finding it lukewarm. Still, she drank it. She needed the kick for the question she was about to ask him. 'Unless there'll be pictures of you coming out like this?'

His gaze didn't waver. 'Heavens no. I prefer brunettes. Mouthy brunettes, to be specific.'

She sat back in her chair and grinned. Couldn't help it. 'We should probably start planning our wedding, then, huh?'

CHAPTER FOURTEEN

THEY LEFT SAN GIMIGNANO that night. They'd spent the afternoon discussing their plan, and they'd both decided going back to South Africa a day early would only benefit them. They could go to Micah's lawyer's offices, sign a prenuptial agreement, and tell her father.

At least, that had been Micah's suggestion. Elena's was more radical.

'We should get married before we tell my father,' she said matter-of-factly. 'There's no point rushing on the pre-nup unless we're getting married soon. And getting married soon will put us in a better position when we see my father.' She glanced at him. 'If you need to buy the parent company of my paper, you can do it for your wife, not your fiancée.'

'I trust you,' he said once he could form a coherent reply. 'I'll do it for my fiancée, too.'

'Yeah. Yeah, it's too fast,' she said, shaking her head. 'Sorry.'

The expression in her eyes had him saying, 'There's more to this, isn't there?' She bit her lip. It tugged at his heart. 'Elena, you can tell me.'

It was a while before she did. 'I'd feel safer—more protected—if we were married when we speak to him.'

It did him in, her vulnerability. He nodded. 'So let's get married before we see him.'

The first half of the plane ride, they spoke about every possible condition they wanted in their pre-nup. Elena's professional independence was assured—at Micah's insistence—as was Micah's wealth—at Elena's insistence. They added clauses about business commitments and personal functions, birthdays and special occasions. They stipulated that neither of them wanted children, and if they did it, both parties would have to agree on it and put it in writing. There would be a probationary period where both of them would have to display the behaviour they wanted to see in a parent. Essentially assuring the other they could do work/home balance.

'Just in case,' Elena said.

'Just in case,' he agreed, but he was sure it wouldn't be necessary.

After they repeated all that and more to their lawyers, who recorded it with their permission, they ended the call and sat staring at one another.

'That was interesting,' he said.

'It was.' There was a beat of silence. 'We didn't talk about sex.'

He paused as he reached for his drink, but continued when he realised he couldn't delay any longer. 'No, we didn't.'

'We'll need to tell them if they need to put an infidelity clause in the contract,' she said nonchalantly. 'I know what you said after the Jameson thing, but if you've changed your mind, we should be prepared for that.'

The way she was picking at her trousers told her she wasn't as relaxed as she was pretending to be.

'I haven't changed my mind,' he said, watching her. 'But I've already had the clause inserted.'

'Yeah?' Her fingers stopped moving. 'What did you say?'

'If I cheat, you can leave.'

She frowned. 'What about me?'

He cleared his throat. 'I told them I would confirm later.'

There was a long pause. She reached over and took the drink from his hands. Unlike him, though, she drank it. He watched her swallow. Only she could make it seem like an action that belonged in a seduction. She pressed the glass to her lips before handing it back to him, as if she'd realised it wasn't hers.

'You know, it's not cheating if we both agree we can go outside the marriage for sex,' she said, watching him closely.

'No, it's not.'

He drank the remaining liquid in one quick gulp.

'We haven't made any decisions about that. Why would you involve the lawyers?'

'I went into this knowing that I didn't want to—' He broke off to clear his throat. Actually, he was giving himself time to figure out what he wanted to say. It wasn't working, so he stopped trying. 'I don't want to go outside our marriage. I know it's not strictly a real marriage, but it feels disrespectful. What if someone saw me and this other woman? The speculation in the media would be as bad as with Jameson.' He shook his head. 'I'm not him.'

'Yet you're telling me *I* can choose that?' She stood and came to sit down next to him. His seat wasn't meant for two, so he ended up half sliding off it. It didn't help; Elena still ended up sitting on him. 'What about the speculation if the media sees me with another man?'

He tried to ignore how wonderful she smelled. How his skin was getting hot and every cell was becoming more aware of her proximity.

'There wouldn't be as much attention on you if you wanted to do that.'

She studied him. 'Stop being so careful, Micah. Tell me what you feel.'

What would it be like to trail a finger over the skin near her collarbone? It looked so smooth, so silky. When they'd been kissing, he hadn't had the benefit of touching her the way he wanted to. He wanted another chance, but in the same breath, he wanted—

'Micah.'

Oh, yes. She was talking to him. 'What?'

She snorted. 'You're being so careful. It's

working on my nerves. I'm sure my questions are doing the same for you.' She didn't wait for an answer. 'I'm going to tell you what I think. Honestly. You might not want to hear it.'

She waited for an answer now, as if he would have one. Should he have one? He tried to ignore the allure of her skin, her collarbone, the memories of that kiss with her, and thought about what she said. She wanted to tell him what she thought about fidelity in marriage. Right. And she wanted to do so honestly because she thought he was being cautious.

He frowned. 'I'm not being careful.'

'You're not saying what you want to say either,' she countered easily, unsurprised by his delayed response.

'I... Elena, I don't know how to say what I want to say.'

'Because you're trying to think like a businessperson. Don't. Think like *you*. A man, a husband, or whatever the hell role will help you to be honest.'

'You really want that?'

'Yes.'

'Fine.' He didn't let himself think. 'I don't want to go outside our marriage for sex for a number of reasons. I've given you a lot of them. The most important is that I find you incredibly attractive, Elena.' His voice dropped. 'I feel…something for you that I have no interest in feeling with anyone else. I doubt I could.' He couldn't help the caress he gave her, starting at that pulse in her neck, tracing the soft skin to her shoulder. 'I don't want to cheat because I don't think I'd want anyone as much as I want you.'

Elena's lips parted, but he didn't think it was only surprise. He had been terribly candid. But the quick breath that pushed through her lips when he skimmed her collarbone told him it was lust, too. She cleared her throat.

'Why would you want me to find someone else then?' Her voice was barely above a whisper.

He put an arm around her waist. When she leaned into him, he pulled her onto his lap. She immediately locked her arms around his neck.

'Did I give you the impression I wanted that?' With her closer now, he could let his lips do the work his fingers had done. He brushed them over that spot at her collarbone. She arched her neck. He kissed the exposed skin. 'Elena, what I want is for you to come to me for your physical needs. But I believe in your independence and your ability to choose what's right for you. If you don't believe in what I believe, I can't fault you for that.'

'Hmm.'

It was all she said. He didn't blame her for the lack of response when he was the reason she wasn't responding. He assumed. His hands were skimming the sides of her breasts now, his thumbs brushing over the light padding of her bra. He didn't linger there—he would lose his mind if he did—but there was no lack of places to touch. She wore a wraparound shirt with her trousers, perfectly respectable as it ended right where her pants started. It was less respectable if someone pushed the end of the shirt up to expose her skin.

He was up for the task.

Her skin was glorious. Soft beneath his touch, the faint strip of brown he'd revealed. She shivered as he touched her, all around her waist, and when he looked at her again, she was watching him with hooded eyes.

'You know,' she said lazily, 'I was going to tell you pretty much the same thing. Not the things about finding you attractive—' she paused to give him a saucy smile '—but that I don't think going outside our marriage for something we could get inside it would be productive for either of us. Of course,' she continued, shifting so that she was straddling him, 'there's an argument that could be made for sex making things murky between us.'

Plump flesh peeked out at him from the V at her chest. He dragged his eyes up.

'Will you be making that argument?'

'I can keep a clear head when it counts,' she told him.

'So, no?'

Her lips curved. 'No. How about you?'

'Please,' he said with a snort.

'Wonderful. Personally, I don't think we should include lawyers in this.' She opened the buttons at the top of his shirt. 'They already know too much about our relationship as is.'

'If you're sure.'

Quite frankly, he didn't care. Not when she was kissing the skin she'd exposed in some sensual tit for tat that he was looking forward to exploring. She sat back at his answer though.

'The way you've handled this whole thing… makes me sure,' she repeated. 'I believe what you say. And I promise I won't cheat on you. I won't break your trust.' She shimmied off his lap, giving him a mild look when he made a noise of protest. 'We should keep things respectable between us until we're married.'

He smiled despite the lust travelling through his veins. 'Should we?'

'Yes.' She sniffed. 'I'm a respectable woman.' She straightened her top and then her shoulders. 'A respectable woman who knows the value of delayed gratification.'

He rested his forearms on his legs, watching her as amusement and dark desire tangled inside him. 'You should tell me more about that.'

With a reflection of his amusement and desire sparkling on her face, she did.

The ethics of marrying a man when she was supposed to announce her engagement to another confused Elena if she thought about it too much. But she was sure it was the right thing to do. If she and Micah didn't get married before they went to speak with her father, she was afraid they never would. She couldn't risk that. This marriage had become a shiny light in a darkness she hadn't realised she'd entered into. It made her feel strong again. She had no idea when she'd lost that feeling, but she had, and to have it back was heady. Especially when she didn't know if it was permanent.

It might be, Elena comforted herself. She might hold on to her strength, her power when they saw her father and told him the news. But the fact that she wasn't sure was enough to make her feel unsteady. Looking at herself in the outfit she was going to get married in didn't make her feel that way though. Nor did the fact that she was about to get married.

Elena stared at herself in the mirror of the hotel suite. They'd arrived in Cape Town hours before, had gone straight to Micah's lawyers and signed their papers. Something had come up for Micah's attention while they were there, and they'd parted, agreeing to meet at the hotel they'd booked a suite in until things were finalised.

She had no idea what that meant, or how it would look, but for illogical reasons it felt like the right thing to do. A part of her expected paparazzi to be at her home, taking pictures of her before she could speak with her father. Or worse, Jameson would be there. Or her *father*. None of that was likely, but she didn't want to worry about that, too. So she accepted Micah's offer of the suite, went to a store and bought herself something to get married in. Then she got ready to get married.

Her outfit of choice was a white suit and lace vest. It was pretty much like the other suits she wore, but fancier. The material was softer, more expensive because it was her wedding day. It was also much sexier than any suit she wore. The lace vest was to thank for that. It covered everything it had to, but it clung, and, with the material like a spider's web, seemed created for temptation.

She felt more comfortable in it than she would a wedding dress, she was sure. And it meant something to her that she wasn't giving up a part of herself to marry someone for her father. Although strictly speaking, she *was* marrying someone for her father. She wouldn't be marrying at all if it weren't for him.

But at least this way he can't weaponise the

fact that you aren't married against you. At least now you're safe.

She hadn't realised how much she'd needed that security until now. She hadn't realised how powerful the threat of her father's presence— the threat of his demands—was in her life. Her heart pained that this was her reality, but it was time she faced it. Just as she had to face that she would rather have the peace of no longer being threatened by her father than the hope of being loved by him. Facing it made her smart. Accepting it would make her happy. At this point, she could only manage the first.

A knock on the door brought her out of her head. Thank goodness. She went to open it.

Micah stared at her dumbly. Shook his head. 'Wow.'

'Hello to you, too,' she said with a smile. It lightened the darkness inside her. Reminded her why she'd agreed to marry him. The light grew when his eyes kept dipping to her outfit. 'You know I have a face, right?'

'Right,' he said, his head snapping up. His eyes widened then, too, and if she didn't think he'd tease her for it, she'd thank him for the reaction. It soothed any remaining shakiness thinking about her father had brought.

'I thought you looked beautiful that night at the banquet. No—I thought you couldn't look *more* beautiful than you did that night at the banquet.' He blinked. 'I was wrong.'

Good heavens, this man was a charmer. She wanted to be annoyed by it, but she couldn't be. The gooeyness slid into her bloodstream, carried to her heart before she could even try.

'Thank you. I'm glad this non-wedding wedding has some wedding wedding elements.'

His eyes grew concerned. 'You know we don't have to do this today.'

She stepped back so he could walk into the room. 'You know we *have* to do this today.'

He brushed a hand against hers as he walked past her. 'Fine. We can have another wedding. A *wedding* wedding.'

'I appreciate the offer, Micah, but I don't want a wedding wedding. The elements of a wedding I want, I have. A man I respect is marrying me. Also someone so completely enthralled by my good looks that he's aware of how lucky he is.'

Micah smiled. 'I guess you do have it, then.

But we can talk about it later. The business thing took longer than expected. We have about twenty minutes before we have to leave for Home Affairs.'

'It's unlikely a government-run department is going to require us to be there on time,' she replied, rolling her eyes.

'Only if you don't have connections.' He winked. 'I'm going to have a shower.'

On his way to the bedroom with its en-suite bathroom, he pressed a kiss to her forehead. Elena spent much too long thinking about the casual gesture. It was just so...*easy.* She didn't completely trust it. Not because she didn't want to; precisely because she wanted to. Whenever things seemed too good to be true, they usually were. At least when it came to Elena and relationships.

She was trying not to think about it when Micah walked into the living room of the suite wearing only a towel. It was like an advertisement, but it was anyone's guess for what. Cotton, for the towel? He was clean-shaven, so it could have been anything to do with shaving. The scent trailing after him was powerful, but not overwhelming, so perhaps he was selling some perfect combination of men's cologne. Or perhaps he was selling nothing. Perhaps his intention had always been to make her salivate.

When they met, she remembered admiring the muscle that was clear in his frame. Now, she could do it first-hand. She'd been right to think there was a layer of softness insulating that muscle. It made Elena wonder why only perfectly sculpted men were used as models. Micah's build made it clear that he was strong and human; he had a life beyond the gym.

As it turned out, that build was *exactly* her type.

And Micah knew it, too.

'Should I worry about the way you're looking at me?' he asked casually.

'Why did you come out of the bedroom if you didn't want me to look at you like this?'

'I'm looking for the suit bag with my clothes in.'

'The one you took into the bedroom?'

He smirked. 'Did I? I must have missed it.' He paused. It felt as though he was giving the electricity between them time to spark. 'I'm not mad about it.'

'I don't imagine you are,' she said in the same mild tone he used. 'Now, get ready so we can go.'

He was smiling when he went back into the bedroom, and when he emerged again minutes later, he looked exactly like the models she wanted to see in fashion campaigns. His suit was tailored to fit his broad shoulders and lean hips, and the navy colour was perfect against his brown skin.

'You look nice,' Elena said when he reached her.

His eyes danced with amusement. 'If that's what your face looks like when I look nice, I might have to call an ambulance to check your heart on days I look gorgeous.'

She rolled her eyes. 'The ego on you.'

'It's not ego when it's the truth.'

'I can't believe I'm marrying someone who said that.'

He offered her an arm. 'Let's make it official anyway.'

She took the arm with a firm grip and a nod that was just as firm. 'Yes. Let's.'

CHAPTER FIFTEEN

MICAH'S CONTACTS ENSURED they were in and out of the Home Affairs office in exactly forty minutes. Married.

They were now married.

Elena refused his offer to get dinner to celebrate. She was worried someone might recognise them and take photos. Those photos would almost certainly reach her father, and they wouldn't have the opportunity to surprise him with the truth.

'It'll be easier if we surprise him, trust me.'

That was all she said until they reached the suite.

He hadn't thought to book two separate rooms for them. Not based on the way they had responded to one another when they'd kissed, or on the plane. Their kiss after they made their vows to one another hadn't been as hot as either of those occasions, but it had lingered, and he'd felt a promise in it. Perhaps that had been presumptuous, but Micah thought he could be on the night of his wedding. Now, he doubted it. Elena had all but curled into herself, and nothing he said lured her out of it.

'Do you want something to eat?' he asked, loosening his tie.

She kicked off her shoes and shook her head. 'No, thank you.'

He didn't think she'd eaten anything since that morning, so he knew she wasn't denying it because she wasn't hungry. He was about to ask when she grabbed her phone and disappeared onto the balcony.

He didn't follow immediately. She needed time and space, clearly. Otherwise, she wouldn't have taken it. But he wanted to follow her. He wanted to demand she talk to him. They were married now, for heaven's sake. He didn't want their marriage to start off on this foot, where they didn't speak with one another.

He had enough of that growing up.

He swore at the reminder.

He'd been avoiding thoughts about his parents since he'd had that revelation about his relationship with his mother. It had been easy to do with everything that had happened in the last few days. But it was still there, as it always was. Lurking around the distractions he offered himself, waiting for an in. Apparently, he'd given it one now.

He threw off his suit jacket and tossed the tie on the bed. He undid his cufflinks and set them on the bedside table. He rolled up his shirt's sleeves, kicked off his shoes, then headed for the minibar in the living room. It was fully stocked, and he grabbed a brandy as he had the night he'd proposed to Elena. Now though, it wasn't to celebrate his actions; it was to clear his thoughts.

His mother would never know about his plan to gain her attention by partnering with Elena's father. That simple fact anchored him. If she knew, he would feel more pathetic than he already did. He was a grown man, and he thought he could get his mother to pay more attention to him through a business transaction. If he had his mother's attention, he wouldn't feel so bad about not having his father's. It would still smart, there was no doubt, but at least he wouldn't feel as abandoned as he did now. Because at least his father had left him for a reason—another family. The kind his father had always wanted, no doubt.

His mother though? She'd left him for a business. For work. Something that had no value in the grand scheme of things.

That very thought told him how much things had shifted in his brain. He'd felt the same way about work as she had for the longest time. Up until this trip to Italy, in fact. In Italy, he'd learnt he could be himself. Have his interests, and still be cared about. He didn't have to twist into impossible shapes for that to happen either. It had just happened, naturally, and it had put a lot of things into perspective.

He was still processing all of it, but he knew this: Elena was his family now. Their marriage might be a business agreement, but their relationship had more emotion in it than anything he'd experienced with his real family. He trusted her, and she wouldn't hurt him the way his mother did. He knew it.

The thought had him stalking to the balcony and opening the sliding doors. He found Elena sitting with her feet against the railing, her phone in her lap.

'It's beautiful, isn't it?' she said before he

could talk. 'I will never forget Italy and everything we saw there, but this? This is…' She
trailed off with a head shake. 'This is home.'

Slowly, he took a seat next to her. The hotel
was in Cape Town's centre, and looked out on
the buildings and streets of the business hub
of the city. They were up high enough that
they could see the ocean during the day. Table
Mountain loomed above it, dark and steady
at night. It didn't have the quietness or the
quaintness that Italy had, but the sounds were
familiar, the stars were brighter and, as Elena
said, it was home.

'I sent Jameson a message telling him I'm
not marrying him.' She wasn't looking at him,
so she didn't see his head whip towards her.
'Then I messaged my father to tell him there
wouldn't be an engagement party tomorrow,
and that I'd see him at eleven a.m. to explain
why. Figured I'd give us some time to have
breakfast, at least.'

No wonder she'd gone quiet.

Even as his instincts congratulated themselves on knowing something wasn't right
with her, his heart chastised him. He'd forgotten about the party. He should have known

saying no to it, to the engagement, would be hard on her. She was worried about disappointing her father, about sacrificing what she wanted from him. Their wedding hadn't only been about them, not for her, and he should have known that.

'How do you feel?'

There was a long silence.

'Good.' She laughed, but it didn't sound free or unburdened. It sounded as if it was wrenched from somewhere deep inside her. 'I feel good. I'm so relieved I made the decision—the right one—and I don't feel like I'm betraying him.'

Her voice changed as she spoke, getting higher and less steady, and he stood and gently pulled her into his arms so she could lean on him.

'No, no, I'm fine,' Elena assured him, but her face was pressed into his chest and he could barely hear her. He was also fairly certain his shirt was wet. 'I'm glad it's you,' she said with a hiccup. She leaned back. She was crying, but she didn't seem to know it was happening. Perhaps she was refusing to acknowledge it.

'I'm *so* glad it's you.' She pressed her lips together. 'This feeling in my chest that used to be there isn't there any more. It feels weird. Empty. Which I know makes no sense because it also feels right.' She curled her hands into his shirt. 'We feel right.'

Now she lifted to her toes and kissed him lightly on the lips.

'I'm so glad it's you,' she whispered again, before wrapping her arms around him and hugging him more tightly than he'd ever been hugged before.

Maybe that was why it felt as if something clicked inside him.

She'd just fixed something broken.

Elena was sure there were rules about not blubbering all over a spouse on the night of a wedding. Too bad. She hadn't paid attention to the rules before when it came to Micah. Though it might have been more accurate to say their relationship hadn't followed the rules since she hadn't actively willed it that way.

She wasn't supposed to feel as though a man she'd met a week ago was the only person she could trust in the world. Trust. It terrified her that she even thought it. There were still parts of her that worried Micah would turn out like her father. Or like any of the powerful men she'd come to know in her life. But she also knew that was unfair. He had proved to her that he was different. Ever since he came to Venice to find her, he'd offered her honesty. He was protecting her. He'd held her when she cried. And when he touched her, he made her head spin and her heart fill.

It was that filling heart that was the *really* scary part about trusting him.

She tried to talk herself out of the fear. Things weren't too good to be true. It was okay to feel safe with him. She didn't have to worry about her father or Jameson or losing her job any more. She would be okay.

'I'm sorry for messing up your shirt,' she said as she pulled back and saw the damage. Smeared make-up and wetness didn't do anything for what she was sure was an expensive piece of clothing. 'I'll pay to have it cleaned.'

'I'll take care of it,' he said. He didn't move closer to her, but it felt as if he wanted to. She had no idea how she knew it. 'Just tell me you're okay.'

'I'm fine.' She walked back into the room. 'It was residual stress from the last few days. Or the last month. I'm fine,' she said again.

'If you're sure.' He was watching her intently. 'Tea?'

'Please.' She watched him go through the motions for a second, then said, 'Who told you to give someone tea when they're feeling shaky?'

He glanced over his shoulder. 'That's a thing?' He smiled when she gave him a look. 'It's part of pop culture. I'm not completely oblivious.'

'Thank goodness for that,' she murmured. She went to the bathroom, washed her face and tied her curls up. She was still wearing her wedding suit, but she had her Italy suitcase with her. She could change into a sleepshirt.

When she left the bathroom, her tea was steaming on the table in the little lounge of their suite. The sleepshirt could wait, she thought, but took off the jacket of her suit and draped it over the back of a chair.

'Thank you,' she said to Micah, who was sitting in the seat opposite the one she'd taken.

'It's a relatively simple way to make you feel better.'

His eyes pierced hers as she took a sip from her tea. She sighed as the warmth soothed the remaining unsteadiness. Then she sighed when she found Micah still looking at her.

'I feel a lot better, I promise. It was really just tension. And all the stuff with my father and Jameson.'

'I understand.' His drink was brown liquor. He sipped it slowly. 'I also understand that you don't always deal with your feelings when they come up, which means something like this happens, I'm betting, quite frequently.'

'No,' she said defensively. 'It's never happened before.'

'Guess I'm wrong then.'

'Not entirely. I mean, I could be better about...' She trailed off. 'This is not a therapy session.'

'It's a hell of a lot cheaper than a therapy session,' he said with a small smile.

'Yeah, I only had to sell my singledom to you. Ooh,' she said when he opened his mouth, 'was that too far? Did I make you feel uncomfortable?'

'No.' He narrowed his eyes. 'I *am* wondering about your sense of humour. That was…dark.'

She laughed. 'Best you know that now before we really get stuck into this marriage thing.'

He smiled, but didn't reply, and they sat drinking their beverages in companionable silence.

'I'm sorry I worried you,' she said softly. 'I wasn't thinking about you… It'll take some time, but I'll get there, I'm sure.

'If it makes you feel any better,' he said in the same tone of voice, 'I wasn't thinking about you either. I should have known marrying me when you had telling your father hanging over your head would be hard.'

'It wasn't—'

'You didn't want to sit on my lap yesterday because of it.' His eyebrows rose. 'Wasn't the respectability about that?'

'Well,' she said, frowning. 'I was doing a little more than sitting on your lap, Micah.'

'I don't remember that.'

There was a challenge in his voice that switched the atmosphere in the room from comfortable to…something else. She couldn't describe what it was, exactly, but it felt dangerous. Not in a *you might get hurt* way, but in an *adrenaline makes you see life differently* way. Suddenly she was aware of the breeze fluttering through the sliding door he hadn't closed. It was a warm night, uncommonly so for the season, so the wind only felt seductive.

She could have been projecting since she also just noticed Micah had unbuttoned the first few buttons of his shirt and rolled up his sleeves. It exposed delicious skin that she wanted to touch. And if she touched, she was certain she would end up wanting more...

'Well,' she said again, setting the empty teacup on the table, 'I can't blame you. I hardly remember it myself. Not the way you touched or kissed me here—' she traced the skin at her neck as he'd done with a finger '—or here.' She touched her midriff, and felt the lace material beneath it.

She wanted to take it off, to offer Micah this piece of her she'd kept guarded for as long as she could remember. But that felt too rash, too brazen. Especially after she'd exposed her emotions to him.

Except that made her feel *more* connected

to him. It made her *want* to be rash, brazen. In the end, she settled for loosening her hair and fluffing the curls. His eyes followed the movement, and his fingers twitched. He wanted to touch them. She wanted him to touch them.

'I don't remember that at all,' he said, setting his own glass down. He stood. Began unbuttoning his shirt. 'I should probably get ready for bed. It'll be a long day tomorrow.'

He pulled the shirt off, revealing the body she'd drooled over earlier that day.

Damn him. He was winning.

'We both should.' She stood and unbuttoned her trousers. Heaven only knew where the modesty she'd felt seconds ago had gone to. Her competitiveness had consumed it.

Her lust had devoured it.

Rash and brazen indeed.

'Is there just this one bed?' she asked, walking past him as she shimmied the trousers over her hips. She'd worn the appropriate underwear for white trousers. She hadn't realised how appropriate it would be for her wedding night. Was that by sheer force of will or ignorance?

'I…er… I didn't think I needed to…'

His words were slow, stammering. She turned around.

'Is something wrong?'

'No.'

But his eyes were sweeping up and down her body. When they rested on her face, the hunger there threatened to steal her breath. The only reason it didn't was because she felt the echo of it inside her. She was playing a game with him, but the truth of it was that she wanted him. Not because of the way he looked without a shirt on, or because of how he wore a suit, or because he looked like the models she'd never had the common sense to conjure.

She wanted him because she wanted to be close to him. She wanted to feel that trust they'd built in a new way. He thought about her as no one had before. He was considerate and cautious, and he wanted her to be independent, to keep her own mind and make her own choices. Despite what he wanted.

It was hugely different from the conditions they'd met under. Or was it? Micah hadn't known her then. He'd been on his own for the longest time, and he didn't know how to think about other people. He hadn't learnt that from his mother since she hadn't shown that to *him*. So he'd emulated what he saw and did what he had been taught. Then Elena had come along, and communicated that honesty, that respect, were important. He'd immediately adhered to that. Though no one had taught him how to consider someone else, he'd done it for her.

That was the man she wanted to make love with. And suddenly her hesitancy, and perhaps even her shame at wanting it, melted away.

'Elena,' he whispered. 'You're so beautiful.'

She bit her lip. 'I don't think you're supposed to say that. Not if you want to win.'

He closed the space between them, his arms resting on her hips. When she didn't shift, the grip of his hands tightened. 'I don't know what competition we were in, but I'm pretty sure I'm winning doing exactly this.'

She circled her arms around his neck. 'I used to think your charm was annoying.'

His head reared back slightly. 'What?'

She chuckled. 'You always knew the right thing to say.'

'And that was annoying?'

'Yes. Because it didn't seem genuine. It seemed…practised.'

'I do *not* practise my charm.'

Again, she laughed at his indignation. 'Of course not. I just meant… It felt like something you had to do. It didn't sound like something you wanted to do.' Her eyes dropped to his lips. 'Now, I know that everything you say comes from you.' She brushed her thumb over his bottom lip. 'The real you, not the person you think you have to be.'

'Elena,' he whispered. 'Let me kiss you.'

She lifted her head to his in response.

CHAPTER SIXTEEN

HE WOKE UP as the sun hit the curtains, the thin material barely keeping the rays of light out. But he didn't mind. He was waking up to a new life, a new world, it felt like. The reason for it lay with her head on his chest, her curls tickling his chin.

Micah ran his finger up and down her spine, his body responding to the touch as much as it did the memories of the night before. He couldn't help but to think about it. To think of her, beneath him, as they made love for the first time. The complete trust on her face, flushed with pleasure. He liked to think he'd earned that flush with the attention he'd lavished on her. The worship of her body—her breasts, her thighs, what lay in between.

When she stirred beside him, he was ready to make new memories.

'Hmm,' she said as he shifted to face her. 'Morning.'

He pressed a kiss to her neck. 'Good morning.'

Her head fell back. 'I think I read an article about this once.'

His kisses made the trail back up until he was kissing behind her ear, a spot he'd discovered she enjoyed quite a bit.

'About this specifically?' he whispered.

'No,' she said with a hoarse laugh. 'It was about marriage. About being careful about what you start your marriage with because your spouse might come to expect it. I think the article was directed at traditionally female roles in the household—don't iron shirts if you don't want to keep doing it, those kinds of things—but it definitely applies now.' Her fingers slipped under his chin. 'Unless you plan on waking me up with seduction every morning, don't do it now.'

'In that case, I should probably give you more realistic expectations.'

He didn't give her a chance to reply before he kissed her. She immediately opened up to him, pressing her body close to him. He gave himself a moment to process the onslaught of sensation. The feeling of her breasts pressed against his chest. Of her skin heating against his. Of the heat of more of her—of *all* of her.

Then he focused on kissing her. He wasn't ever going to tire of it. Good thing, too, because the more he kissed her, the more responsive she became. The hand that wasn't caught beneath her trailed down his back, lingering, caressing. When it moved to his front, reaching between them, he heard the groan as if it came from outside himself.

The touches, the kisses, the intense intimacy. The emotion, the connection, the feeling of only *them*. All of it made him feel as if he were floating above his body. Then she welcomed him into hers, and he dropped back to earth, overwhelmed by pleasure and gratitude for his wife. His partner. His…equal.

After, Elena told him to shower first so she could call down for breakfast. As the water beat down on him, he pondered his thoughts during their lovemaking. Explored how they made him feel. It was strange, but there was no alarm. Only an odd kind of acceptance. This was his life now. Elena was his wife, his partner, his equal. It was a life he'd never contemplated, and now, he couldn't imagine it being any different.

He left the bathroom with a bemused smile—which immediately faded when he saw Elena. She was standing in a hotel robe, phone in her hand, a tight expression on her face.

'I put it on to check if my father called.' Her voice was disturbingly detached. 'He did. I didn't listen to the voicemails, but I have a message that says I'd better have an explanation.'

He walked over and pulled her into his arms. 'We knew this was going to happen, Elena. Your father was never going to accept the embarrassment of cancelling an engagement party without an explanation.'

'Even *with* an explanation he might not.' She was chewing her thumbnail even as her head rested on his chest. 'I know we expected this. I just…'

She didn't finish her sentence, only pulling away from him to look out through the sliding door.

'Elena?'

She took a deep breath. 'This is going to be hard.'

He shoved his hands into his pockets. She'd moved away from his physical offer of comfort, and he didn't know if he should keep trying. He didn't know if he had the right to. It was a confusing thought to have after what they'd shared the night before, that morning. After his thoughts in the shower. But he didn't know if a spouse or partner or equal meant… Well, this. Emotional comfort, he supposed, though that didn't feel like an adequate explanation.

It was all clouded, muddled, so he focused on what was clear.

'It is going to be hard.'

She gave him a shrewd look. 'I'm pretty sure you're supposed to say something more supportive than that.'

He curved his lips, but it wasn't a smile. 'I *am* being supportive. If I tell you it'll be easy, you'll know it's a lie. At least this way, we can prepare for hard.'

'We?'

He shrugged, though her question felt as if it clouded things even more. 'We're partners, aren't we?' He didn't wait for an answer. 'I'm expecting this to be like a business meeting. A particularly difficult one, but a business meeting nevertheless. We're offering him the reality of our situation. The way he engages with that is his problem.'

She kept biting her nail. He took a step forward. Stopped.

'Elena, look at me.' Her eyes lifted. 'You don't have to be afraid of him.'

'Don't I?' she asked in a small voice.

'You're married to a man who's just as powerful as your father is. Maybe more. Externally,' he clarified. 'But *you're* the person who's dealt with him your entire life, despite being afraid of him, and come out on the other side.' He couldn't resist walking to her now, or tipping up her chin. 'That takes courage. You've built a successful career outside him. That takes strength. You're kind and sharp and annoyingly quick-witted—' he smiled when her eyes narrowed a fraction '—and that makes you just as powerful as he is. More.'

Her eyes filled, and she bit the bottom of her lip when it started to tremble. Then, in movements quicker than he could anticipate, she rose to her toes and gave him a passionate kiss. She pressed her body into his, wrapping her arms around him and tightening them so much he thought she was trying to become a part of him.

But she already has.

The thought had him breaking off the kiss, pulling away. He was panting, but he didn't know if it was from her or from the shock of that thought.

She gave him a little nod, acknowledging his response in some knowing way, before disappearing into the bathroom. Micah stared after her for a long time.

What did she think she knew? And why did he feel as if that would change things more than any realisation he had about their relationship?

It was hard to imagine that once upon a time, she'd lived in this house with her parents. She'd thought she had a good life. A normal life. But she hadn't known then that mothers didn't tend to be as cool with their children as her mother had been with her. She hadn't known that most children didn't feel as though they needed to earn their parents' love and approval. That fathers didn't treat their children as objects.

Her parents' divorce had changed many things, but most of all, it had opened her eyes. And when she'd started seeing, something had cracked open inside her. Nothing had been able to fill that crack. Not friendships, though she didn't have enough of those to judge. Not her job, though she'd tried her hardest for it to. But this morning, when Micah had been tenderly outlining all the things that meant she could take on her father, Elena had felt the crack fill.

She was forced to face it then. Forced to face what she'd been running from since Italy.

She was in love with him.

It was concerning in many ways. They'd known one another for just over a week. A *week*. She scoffed at people who claimed to fall in love so quickly. Now, she wanted to talk to them all and ask them how it was possible. Did they fall for the other person's sincerity? Their willingness to change? Did they fall for the efforts their person made *to* change?

Or was it the quiet determination their partner vowed to protect them with? Or the passionate tenderness they made love with?

Was it just that Micah was this way? That he was the person she was meant to be with? That falling in love with him was simply inevitable?

She couldn't deny they'd had a connection from the moment they met. Getting married had sealed that bond. Sleeping together had solidified it. Deepened it. In between the pleasure and sighs, Elena's world had changed and she didn't know what to do about it.

Especially when she was sure Micah's world had stayed the same.

Micah squeezed her hand. She looked over, realised he'd been watching her. He thought the turmoil on her face was because they were about to see her father. Tension skittered through her body. Yes, this meeting was more pressing than her feelings. She'd have to put off dealing with falling in love with her husband until *after* she'd dealt with the first man whose love she wanted, but would never receive.

She stilled. Then nausea welled inside her

and she had to exert every ounce of control to ignore it.

They walked to the large house that had been painted from white to grey since she'd moved out. She hadn't been here since. Then her father summoned her to his office and now here she was. She should never have answered the call.

The area in front of the house had been designed around a circle. Trees and bushes formed the inner and outer circle, with gravel filling the spaces in between. There was already a car parked on the gravel when they arrived, and it took her all of two seconds to recognise it as Jameson's. Her father's cars would be parked in the garage at the back of the house. Something rebellious inside her had almost guided Micah there as well, but she resisted. She didn't understand why she felt disappointed that she had.

'You okay?' Micah asked as they rang the doorbell. He spoke under his breath, as if he was worried someone would hear. Clever. She wouldn't put it past her father to put a camera at the door so he could watch unsuspecting guests.

'Good.' Her voice cracked.

'Do you want me to do this alone?'

At that, she turned. Gave him a faint smile. 'I have to do this. I have to.' She spoke as much to herself as she did to him.

He opened his mouth, but the door opened before he could.

'Elena,' the woman at the door said when she saw them, her eyes going wide.

'Rosie,' Elena said, not quite believing it. 'You're still here.'

She walked into the open arms of the John housekeeper, feeling a warmth she'd missed since they'd started preparing for the meeting. Rosie had always been kind to her, though professional—her parents wouldn't accept anything else—and Elena hadn't seen her since she'd left either.

'Of course I'm still here.' Rosie's voice still held the traces of her native country. 'You would have known that if you'd come to visit.'

'You know why I haven't,' Elena said, the warmth dimming. 'It wouldn't have gone well for either of us.'

'I see,' Rosie said, her eyes tight. 'Well,

child, you've grown up well. I am happy about that, if nothing else.'

'And I'm happy you *are* still here. I thought your sharp mouth would have got you into trouble.'

Elena was teasing, but it was a legitimate concern. Rosie meant well, but she was too honest. She spoke her mind even when she wasn't asked, though that had been reserved for Elena's ears. But with no one else listening, Elena had wondered if her father had been a recipient of Rosie's comments. If he had been, there would not have been the same indulgence.

'My mouth is not so sharp these days.' Her eyes were, though, and they told Elena Rosie had learnt that lesson the hard way. Her heart beat painfully, but she managed a smile.

'I hope it'll still be with me.'

'Child, you are supposed to announce an engagement today. Your husband will have a sharp mouth to put you in your place.'

'There it is.' A relieved laugh tickled Elena's throat, but despite the reprieve from her tension, she wasn't in the mood to laugh. 'Actually, that's why I'm here. To introduce my father to my husband.'

She gestured to Micah. He held out his hand, smiling as charmingly as he'd been taught. But before he could speak, a voice thundered from the top of the stairs.

'What the hell did I just hear?' A tall, stately man descended, but stopped after three steps. 'Did you say this man is your husband?'

Elena's breath left her for a second. Somehow, despite it, she managed a small, 'Yes, Dad. This is my husband.'

Micah wanted to throttle the man who made Elena's voice change like that. From warm to cool; from strong to almost broken. He'd hated everything about the last hours they spent together. She'd barely spoken to him, the fire that was essential to her nowhere to be found.

If he thought it was only because of her father, he would have understood. But something about the way he caught her looking at him—the way she quickly looked away when he did—made him think this had to do with *him*. It was easier to blame her father. Easier than examining everything he'd done, trying to figure out what had made her respond this way.

He forced himself into the present. Elena's father was coming down the stairs, followed by a man Micah recognised as her would-be fiancé. The man's gaze was on him: a sharp, accusatory stare that didn't bother Micah a single bit. If looks had any effect on him, he wouldn't have been the man he was, nor the businessperson.

'Please explain to me why you're saying you're already married when we're supposed to announce your engagement tonight?' Cliff John asked stonily.

Elena's shoulders hunched slightly. Rosie inched forward, as if to comfort Elena, but Elena shot her a look and the woman left the room, shaking her head. Micah shifted closer to Elena, just a fraction, so she could feel him by her side. No matter what was going on between them, he would show his support. That was what their marriage was about.

She cleared her throat. 'Dad, this is Micah Williams. He's the man I was doing the story on for the newspaper.' Elena turned to him.

'Micah, this is my father. Cliff John. And this is…' She faded, then shook her head, her shoulders straightening again. A fierce pride shot up inside him. 'This is Jameson St Clair.'

He waited until both men were level with them before moving over the gleaming white tiles to offer his hand.

'Mr John. I've heard a lot about you.'

He left it at that. Cliff John stared at him for a moment, but took his hand. Micah turned to Jameson. He didn't offer a hand, but gave the man a slight nod.

'Mr St Clair.'

He moved back to Elena's side immediately.

'Elena, is it true?' Jameson asked before Micah got there. 'You're married to him?'

'Yes.'

Elena stared at him in a mixture of defiance and strength. Micah resisted his smile, but welcomed the enjoyment. *This* was his Elena. This was his wife.

'Explain yourself, Elena,' Cliff said. 'I won't ask again.'

Micah ground down on his teeth to keep from responding. He waited for Elena—they all did. She was quiet for a long time, though her defiance and strength didn't falter. She didn't need his protection, he realised. Perhaps externally, as he said, but not where it mattered.

'I didn't want to marry Jameson,' she said eventually. Simply. 'You didn't give me much of a choice, so I had to create one for myself.'

'So you married *him*?' Jameson snapped. 'The man I told you was using you to get to your father?'

Micah did his best not to look at Elena, but he understood why her anger had been so fierce now. She had every right to be angry, regardless of how she had found out, but finding out from Jameson? From another man using her? It must have stung. Micah would have done anything to go back and change his motives. He didn't want to be on the list of men who'd tried to use her.

'It isn't so different from how you wanted to use me, is it? At least Micah had the decency to care about me.'

'I can't imagine why you thought you didn't have a choice, Elena.' Her father's voice was disinterested, as were his eyes, but Micah wasn't fooled. His lips were thinned under his white moustache, the skin between his eye-brows furrowed. Micah was good at reading people, and Cliff John was upset.

No, not upset. Livid.

He could feel Elena tremble at his side, but her chin lifted. 'You threatened my job.'

'Did I?' Cliff asked, edging forward. Elena moved back, without realising it, he was sure. Micah shifted, too, but he wished with all his strength he'd stood behind her so she would have backed into him and realised what she was doing.

'I thought I was merely offering you something you've always wanted: to make me happy,' Cliff continued.

Micah felt the change in Elena's body at that statement. The trembling stopped; *everything* stopped. She didn't move, didn't blink, didn't breathe. Just when he thought he would have to intervene, she exhaled sharply. Her inhalation was just as sharp. She looked at Micah, and the emotion there, along with everything else he'd witnessed over the last few minutes, handed the baton over to him.

'And she still is, Mr John,' Micah said smoothly. 'Elena conveyed your intentions regarding the marriage you proposed.' Disgust coated his tongue at that line, but he continued. 'We believe we can still reach those ends with different means.'

Micah didn't spare a glance at Jameson when the man snorted. He had Cliff's attention. And if he had it, Elena didn't. She could process whatever was happening in her brain.

He angled his head. 'You've probably already heard of me, Mr John, but I'll assume you haven't and tell you who I am.' He didn't pause at the slight rise of Cliff's eyebrows. 'I sell a lifestyle to all of Africa. Recently, I've expanded to Europe. I don't have to tell you what a partnership between my business and yours could mean for both of us.' He let it linger. 'But mostly for you.'

'You're arrogant.'

'Confident,' Micah corrected. Then smiled. 'Perhaps arrogant suits, too. It's semantics, honestly. Would you like to discuss semantics, Mr John, or would you like to discuss how I can make John Diamond Company the talk of the diamond industry? Not only in Africa, but the world?'

'You can't do that,' Jameson said, speaking

for the first time since Micah started his pitch. 'John Diamond Company existed long before you and your business. What can a partnership with you do for their profile that they couldn't do themselves?'

'I imagine it's the same thing a partnership with your family could do for them.' He still didn't look at Jameson directly, because he knew it would annoy the man and impress Cliff. 'Except on a much larger scale. I just signed a contract with the second biggest jewellery store chain in Italy. The contract was based on me providing them with diamonds from Africa that are reliable, well known and ethically sourced. I was hoping you'd be my supplier, but, if not, I'd be happy to offer the opportunity to someone else.'

Micah experienced the stunned silence with the same satisfaction he did every successful business deal. He was certain he'd won Cliff John over. He wouldn't need to secure Elena's job—although he'd already put out feelers to do that, if necessary—because Cliff had come over to their side. His daughter's disobedience had brought damn near world domination for his company right to his doorstep. He wouldn't dare do anything to make her unhappy now.

It wasn't the emotional support Micah wanted to offer her that morning, but it was the best he could do.

'Mr Williams—may I call you Micah?' Cliff's tone had eased into a charm he was willing to bet was Cliff's 'closer' voice.

'Of course. We are family.'

'Micah.' Cliff's smile was all teeth. 'Why don't you come up to my office and we can discuss this in more detail?'

Micah turned to Elena. Her expression was closed, but that wasn't unsurprising if she was still processing. 'Would you like to come with?'

'No,' she said softly. She smiled at him, but it didn't reach her eyes. Alarm fluttered through him. 'No, thank you. I don't have anything to add to that conversation.' Elena waved a hand. 'I'll see you at home.'

'You're leaving?'

'Only because it's business.' She leaned forward and brushed a kiss on his cheek. Then she turned to her father. 'I assume this is fine with you?'

Her voice was cool and, again, pride filled him. She was fighting back. He knew it cost her, but they would deal with that together.

'Perfectly fine.'

'You asked me to be here, Cliff,' Jameson said, all rage. 'You told me we'd get to the bottom of this misunderstanding. How am I supposed to explain this to everyone? What am I supposed to do with everything we've bought and planned for today?'

'I'll cover any financial costs you've incurred,' Micah said, looking away from Elena to Jameson. 'It's the least I can do.'

'You son—'

'Jameson,' Cliff interrupted. His voice was a mirror of the coldness of Elena's, and stopped Jameson in his tracks. 'I think it's clear there hasn't been a misunderstanding. I'll make sure people believe the engagement was only rumours. When they announce the marriage to the world, all will be forgiven.'

'Wh—what about me?' Jameson asked, eyes wide. 'What about my family's company?'

'This is business,' Cliff said, his smile shark-like. 'Deals fall through every day.'

Jameson stared at them, stunned. Elena broke the silence.

'I think I'll get Rosie to call me a car.'

She left all three men with that. Micah stared after her, willing her to look back, to acknowledge their win. She didn't.

CHAPTER SEVENTEEN

ELENA SPENT THE ride to the hotel wondering what she was going to do next.

The suite was booked for another night, but she couldn't bear to stay there again. She cherished the memories that had been created there. She'd got ready for her wedding there. She'd talked and laughed and made love to her husband there. She had never felt closer to another person than she had in that room.

It would be a constant reminder that she was in love with Micah and he would never be in love with her.

She might have been overreacting. But as she'd watched him go to bat for her she'd realised two things. One, she loved him even more deeply than she first thought she did. He protected her exactly as he said he would. More importantly, he supported her. His steady presence, his proximity... All of it had given her the courage to finally stand up to her father. To finally see, *truly* see, the extent of how her father was using her.

Cliff knew that she wanted his love and approval and he'd used that against her. A man like that didn't deserve Elena's love and attention. It hurt more than she could possibly express, but she had been clinging to her father for too long. To the hope that he would love her because if he didn't, who else would? Not her mother, who had forgotten Elena existed years ago. Elena didn't have friends, or other family members. She had a husband, but her second realisation told her he wouldn't love her either. Because as she watched him handle the situation with her father, she knew he was perfectly happy with the arrangement they'd made.

Their *business* arrangement. Not a marriage, but a partnership. She couldn't live with him, sleep with him, love him knowing that he would only ever see it that way.

She'd spent her entire life trying to get one man to love her. She couldn't spend the rest of it trying to do the same with another.

She pressed her lips together as she packed her belongings into her bag and called a car.

She was about to grab her wedding outfit in the garment bag in the closet, but stopped. It would only hurt her to see it. For it to remind her that she loved her husband and needed him to love her back, but he didn't. Without a backward glance, she left the room and went to her home.

When she was there, she opened her laptop to check her emails. She'd been avoiding work and the implications of her marriage for much too long. Micah hadn't replied to the email about her story, so she assumed he had no notes. Not that it mattered. There was no way she could write the story as his wife.

Her heart broke as she outlined the information for her boss, attaching what she had written so whoever got assigned to the story would benefit from her trip to Italy. She'd come back the day before, yet it felt like a dream. The exploration, the privacy, the newness. Now she was back home, feeling more exposed than she ever had, by a situation she shouldn't have put herself in.

The response from her editor—that was somehow a rebuke, congratulations, and request in one—told her to focus on work. It was reliable. And with Micah as her husband, her job was safe. She closed her eyes. Shook her head. Focused. She might have messed up her old assignment, but she wouldn't mess up this new one. She would write about her whirlwind courtship with Micah for the newspaper. It would be more fiction than fact, but the readers would never know. And they would love it. If they did, this could still be a way forward for her.

She wrote back, then got up to make herself a cup of tea. She was nursing it on her couch when the knock on the door came.

She'd been expecting it. With one last sip of her tea, she set it on the coffee table and opened the door.

'Elena?' Micah walked in, moving in for a kiss. She assumed. She stepped back before he could touch her. She wouldn't torture herself with more memories. 'Are you okay? Your things weren't in our room when I got back.'

'You found me,' she said easily, closing the door behind him. 'Do you want tea? Coffee? I don't keep alcohol in the house. I'm sorry about that.'

'No.' His brow was creased so deeply she

was sure there would be indentations once it smoothed. 'I want to know if you're okay.'

'No.' She went to sit on the couch again, bringing her tea with her and crossing her legs. 'But I will be.'

He didn't move a muscle, just kept standing there. She could almost see inside his brain. He was trying to work out what to say. Going through everything that had happened to check whether something had gone wrong.

He wouldn't be able to see it. He hadn't done anything wrong; *she'd* been the one to change. She was no longer happy with their arrangement. She needed him to love her. She needed the person she was in love with to love her. The fact that he didn't would torment her every day. She'd do everything in her power to try and change his mind. She knew she would because that was what she'd done with her parents. With her father. And look where that had brought her.

Micah didn't deserve that. He didn't deserve her trying so hard to please him she lost herself. He'd made his arrangement with her; not the version of her that she thought he wanted.

Beyond that, Elena finally saw that *she* didn't deserve it. She deserved to be fulfilled and happy. She deserved to be herself.

'What's going on in your head, Elena?' Micah asked eventually.

'We made a mistake,' she said softly.

'What do you mean?' He moved now, sitting on the chair opposite her. His body was stiff.

'Last night,' she forced herself to say. 'Sleeping together. We shouldn't have done that.'

'Why not?'

She fortified her heart at the curt words.

You expected this. But if you don't do it now it'll be worse.

'I was right. It made things murky.'

'Is that supposed to make sense to me?' He stood. She merely lifted her chin. She wouldn't get up. Her knees wouldn't hold her. 'What are you saying? What are you *really* saying?'

She didn't know how to respond to his anger. She was already feeling vulnerable, and every word he said battered against her defences. She wanted to tell him that she loved him, that she wanted him to love her, but she couldn't stand to be rejected. Not after hearing her father use her love for him against her. Not after figuring out her feelings for Micah. It was all too much.

But she could do this. She could get through this. She had with her father, and she would now. After a few more breaths, she said, 'We have a business arrangement, and it works. We both got what we wanted from my father today. We'll likely continue to be successful working together in the future. But sleeping together adds a dimension to this relationship that…that won't work.' She took another breath. 'Business, Micah. Let's keep it that way.'

It was clawing at him, the familiarity of this situation. But the claws came from a dark place. He couldn't afford to shine a light on it when he needed all his attention to understand Elena. Her posture was stiff and cold, worse than it had been when they'd been at her father's. Her face was beautiful in its aloofness, he could admit, but he didn't like it. He preferred the beauty of her smiles, the animation in her eyes. When she was teasing him, or gazing at him with lazy pleasure. He wanted *his* Elena back, not the one who brought the claws and destroyed the light. The one he didn't understand.

'Why?'

'I told you—'

'You gave me some rubbish diplomatic answer,' he hissed. 'I want to know *why*? What changed between last night—this morning—and now?'

He realised he sounded desperate, but he couldn't help it. Panic had joined his complicated emotions, spurring the words.

Slowly, she set her tea down on the table in front of her. It was a round glass table held up by metal spirals painted gold. What a strange thing for him to note. Especially when his eyes shifted to her hands and he could see them shaking.

'I'm doing this to...to protect us.'

'From what?'

'From me.'

She blinked rapidly, showing emotion she hadn't given him since he'd come to find her. He thanked the universe for it. Emotion was what made *his* Elena, and if she was showing it, even in this form, it meant that she was coming back. If she came back, maybe this wasn't some warped repetition of his childhood.

He didn't have a chance to process that thought.

'I spent my life trying to get my father to love me because he's the only person I thought would.' A tear ran down her cheek, but her gaze was steady on him. Strong. 'A mistake. He showed me a fraction of approval once and I mistook it for love. I based all my hope on it.' She shook her head. Cleared her throat. 'I… I can't do the same thing with you, Micah.'

Her words paralysed him.

His thoughts kept running though. The panic kept fluttering. But now he saw it was for a completely different reason. Before, it had been because he was worried she would reject him—them. Now, he was worried she was about to change them. For ever.

'You're happy with the way things are between us.'

'I… Yes. It's *us*,' he said, his voice cracking towards the end.

'I'm not,' she replied softly. 'I want more

from you. I *need* more. Can you give me more?'

He opened his mouth, but the claws were back, threatening to shred his tongue if he replied.

'It's okay,' she said, voice hoarse. 'It wasn't a fair question. I shouldn't have asked it.'

'Elena.' He shook his head. 'What are you saying?'

'You know what I'm saying.' She stood now, squaring off with him in a raw way that broke his heart. 'I can't say it. I won't say it, and complicate the arrangement we have.' She continued without letting him speak. Which was good. He had nothing to say. 'I'll keep to the agreement. I'll attend social functions, or business functions. Have Serena sync our social diaries and send me information and I'll be the perfect spouse.'

'I don't…expect you to do something you don't want to do.' He spoke slowly. Heard the emptiness of it. 'I won't use you like they did.'

'You won't be using me,' she said, shoulders straightening. 'We have a contract.'

'I won't keep to the contract.'

She stiffened. 'I'm a woman of my word.'

'If you were a woman of your word, you wouldn't be changing the terms of this relationship on me,' he spat. He knew he'd regret it later. Didn't care.

'Do you think I want this?' she demanded, ice melting into fire. 'I want to focus on healing after this whole thing happened with my father. I want to stay your friend, or whatever the hell we are, Micah. That's what I *want*. But the one thing isn't possible with the other. I can't be your friend if I want to heal.'

'I'm not your father.'

'No, you're my husband. But you can't love me in the same way he can't love me, so what does it matter? I can't live the rest of my life like that.' Her tears reappeared, but she ignored them. 'How can I live the rest of my life wanting someone to love me *again*? How does that help me heal?'

He took a breath, wanting to say words that would make them both feel better. But he couldn't. He was afraid, and the fear pulsed so loudly, he couldn't hear what words they were. He could only hear the warnings, could only feel the alarm. He said nothing.

'See?' she said softly. 'I was trying to protect us by giving you an easy way out. Now we're just in pieces.'

Slowly, so slowly, he walked to her door. 'Elena,' he said, turning around. 'I'm sorry. I want to—'

'Don't,' she interrupted. 'I understand. You can't love me because if you do, it makes you as vulnerable to me as you are to your parents. They've caused you enough pain. At least this way, you don't have to worry that I'll do to you what your parents did to you.'

His world stopped for a second. As it did, the darkness overtook his senses and he saw she was right. But it didn't matter because, now, *he* wanted to protect himself. To fight back the darkness, the fear, and crush the claws. He couldn't do that with her. She would remind him that he wasn't as strong as she was. She would remind him of a light he could never possess.

With one last look, he walked away from his wife.

CHAPTER EIGHTEEN

ELENA MIGHT HAVE got married, but her life was as normal as it had been before her wedding. Apart from the fact that she had to pretend to be living a blissful, married life, of course. Her editor had read her piece on her and Micah's marriage, had decided it would be a great companion piece to the profile Elena had done on Micah, and printed both. One on the front page of the business section; the other on the front page of the entertainment section.

Separation from her husband had no part in that. So Elena lived the lie.

No one would know it wasn't the truth. Micah's profile was high enough that no one expected him to carpool with her to work or pop in for lunch. Micah certainly wouldn't tell anyone. Things would become more complicated if there was an event Micah was at and Elena wasn't at his side. But it had been six weeks and that hadn't come up yet. She would worry about it if it did. In the meantime, she would enjoy the boost those articles had given her career.

After some adjustments, apparently. Her new workload had been a welcome distraction from her emotions, but it had left her feeling run-down. She was tired all the time, even when she woke up, and she had no appetite. It was more or less the same way her body had responded to the adjustment of boarding school, and then the school nurse had done some tests and prescribed some vitamins. She'd felt so much better afterwards though, so she forced herself to go to the doctor even though she had no time for it. She wasn't as understanding when they called to discuss the results.

'Doctor, I'm sure you have a lot of things to do today other than tell me my iron is low.' Elena offered the woman a winning smile. 'We can make this quick.'

'I appreciate the offer,' Dr Jack said dryly,

'but it's a little more complicated than an iron problem.'

'Oh?' She sat up straighter. 'No anaemia? Some other vitamin deficiency, then?'

'None of the above.' Her expression was kind. 'You're pregnant.'

'I'm—' Elena broke off with a laugh. 'Please. There's no way I'm…'

She trailed off when she realised there was a way. A very logical way, really, since she wasn't on anything and condoms were…

'Are you sure? I haven't had unprotected sex.'

'I am sure. This indicates you're about seven weeks pregnant?' Dr Jack showed her some page with levels of hormones, which she honest to goodness couldn't take in. 'If you tell me when your last period was, I'll be able to tell you more accurately. I also have an ultrasound machine in my examination room. If you'd like more certainty, we can do that?'

Elena nodded numbly. She did everything numbly after that. Except when the doctor smoothed gel over her belly, pressed the wand against her stomach, adjusted some things on the machine, and a heartbeat sounded in the small room.

A heartbeat. That was coming from inside her.

'That sounds good,' Dr Jack said, examining the machine. She tilted it towards Elena. 'This is your baby. They're still a small little thing at this point, which is normal based on how far along you are. Seven and a half weeks now that I have that information about your period.'

'But...the sex was...'

She couldn't finish that with the heartbeat still pumping. It was so fast. Was that normal?

'Well, we count based on the first day of your last period, though conception might take place later. Don't tell anyone I said so, but it's hard to say accurately.' There was a pause, and then the sound disappeared. Dr Jack set the wand back at the machine and sat down beside her. 'I can tell by your reaction that this is a surprise. I can talk to you about your options. I can also give you a copy of this so you can listen to it later when you're deciding about your options.'

'That seems a bit harsh, Doctor,' Elena managed to say. 'Am I supposed to make a decision while listening to...to that?'

Dr Jack smiled. 'You don't have to listen to it. I just want you to have the option of listening to it. Now, let's get you cleaned up here and have a conversation about what's going to happen next, shall we?'

'Mrs Williams? Mrs Williams, please.'

For a moment Micah wondered what Serena was doing calling his mother. But Elena was already in front of him before his brain could figure out the calling was happening inside his office.

'I'm sorry, Micah. She wouldn't listen to me.'

'I have to talk to you,' Elena said, looking a little wild.

He took her in—greedily, though he would never admit it—and made sure she was okay. Then he gave a little nod to his PA and waited until the door was shut.

'Wait, why did Serena call me Mrs Williams? She calls me Elena.'

'You've let the world know we're married, haven't you?' He clung to the coolness, though everything inside him yearned to hold her. 'Why have you barged into my office in the middle of a workday?'

She frowned. Shimmied her shoulders. 'I have to talk to you.'

He merely lifted his eyebrows.

'It's important.'

He tried not to let his concern show. It was tough, particularly since he'd spent most of the last six weeks wondering how she was. Even when he managed to bury it by burying himself with work, it popped into his thoughts. When he was in a meeting, or walking to one. When he got home and headed to bed and wondered what it would have been like to come home to her. To have her waiting in his bed.

Those thoughts flooded his mind more and more as the days passed. It would have forced him to face what was keeping them from being together even if his parents hadn't suddenly contacted him. His mother had reached out when she'd heard about his partnership with Cliff John. It had been less than he'd hoped for, but more than he'd expected. She'd arrived at his office, primly asked him out to dinner.

When he'd accepted, she'd spent the evening talking about work. They had nothing else in common, he supposed, and still he'd longed for more. He hadn't heard from her since, and he had no desire to reach out from his side either.

It took a while to accept it, but he realised it had been in motion from the moment he'd proposed to Elena. He knew then already that the reunion with his mother would underwhelm him. It had tempered his expectations, hence the surprise at her offer of dinner. He'd been even more surprised when his father had congratulated him on his marriage. Micah hadn't read the profile Elena's newspaper had done on him, uninterested in reliving Italy when his memories of her feistiness, her laugh, her kiss there kept him awake at night.

Apparently, the article had been combined with an article on their whirlwind courtship and marriage. His father had relayed that fact; Micah hadn't read that article either. When his father asked if Micah and Elena wanted to join him and his wife for dinner some time, Micah told him he would get back to him. He never had. One, he and Elena weren't doing anything together any more. Two, if his father only wanted him to join his family for supper when he was a married man… Yeah, he could stuff that invitation.

His dream about reconciling with his parents had come true in the last weeks, and he was unhappy. Because he saw how damaging that dream was—how damaging *they* were. They'd taught him that opening his heart would only hurt him. Even when he wanted to open his heart, fear of disappointment kept him from doing so.

Screw them.

'Are you going to tell me this important thing?'

'It's better if I show you.'

Elena didn't seem deterred by his sharpness. He was annoyed that he wanted her to be. That he wanted to affect her in the same way she affected him.

She wanted a real relationship with you. What more do you want?

Anger and frustration—at himself—kept him from answering that question. It didn't stop his inhalation when she came to his side of the desk, putting a flash drive into his computer. He was a masochist, probably, but he wanted to see if he'd remembered her smell correctly. He had. It was still as soft and tempting as it had been that week in Italy.

That night in their hotel room.

'I have no idea what this is, but—'

A rhythmic sound stopped his words in their track. It was fast, loud—a *da-da,da-da,da-da* that went on and on and on. His eyes lifted to the screen of his computer. It was black and grey, but the grey was in a strange shape that—

Oh. His brain put the sound and the screen together and… Oh. *Oh.*

'What are we going to do about this?' Elena croaked at him. He looked at her. She was watching the screen, looking as helpless as he felt. 'It's a…a…'

'A baby.'

Now she looked at him. 'Yeah. A baby. That we made.' She laughed in a way that clearly indicated she didn't find it funny. 'Micah, we made a *baby.*'

A string of questions ran through his mind. *Are you sure? How sure? How did you find*

*out? Are you okay? Is the baby okay? How
are we going to be parents?*

He got stuck on the last one, mainly because
he thought Elena was, too. The other questions were kind of already answered by her
appearance there. Of course she was sure—
she wouldn't have been there otherwise. She'd
found out from a doctor; he was looking at the
evidence of that. And he was sure she would
have told him by now if they weren't okay. She
wouldn't have asked what they were going to
do about it if they weren't…would she?

'Are you both okay?'

'Yeah, we're fine.' She exited the window
on the computer, as if she was done watching
the grey and black and hearing the *da-da,da-
da,da-da*. 'I'm tired, and eating's a problem,
which is why I went to the doctor in the first
place, but I'm fine otherwise. And things seem
normal with the…you know.' She shrugged.
'It's early.'

He got stuck on one piece of information.
'You're nauseous?'

'No. I just…don't want to eat. I doubt that
has anything to do with the pregnancy. I for-

got to ask, actually. I guess I'll have to read up on it.'

'What else could it have to do with?'

She quirked a brow. 'Really? That's what you want to talk about?'

'I'm still processing the other thing.'

Her expression softened. 'Stress. I've been working a lot. The…um…the articles about you helped.'

Are you working a lot because of me? Because you're trying to forget me the same way I'm trying to forget you?

It was presumptuous, but he was sure that was why.

It wasn't only presumptuous though. It was unfair. She was the one who'd taken a risk. She had put her feelings out there, hoping for something more. He couldn't give her more.

Except apparently, he had. If she was keeping the baby, they'd be as linked by their child as they were by their marriage contract. More. They could ignore their marriage contract. They'd been doing that for six weeks now. They couldn't ignore their child.

They were going to have a child.

'Can I help?' he asked, a little woodenly.

'The stress probably isn't great for the baby. So. Can I help in some way?'

'Oh. No. Not unless you can write my stories for me.'

'I can get you an assistant to—'

'It's okay, Micah. I can manage.'

'With the baby?' he asked. 'Are we keeping it?'

'We?'

He looked at her. She didn't show any emotion, and he realised she was protecting herself. 'You don't need me, I know. But this is *our* responsibility.'

'When did I ever say I didn't need you?' she asked, a flicker of angst crossing her face before it was gone. 'I'd like to keep it. I... I don't know anything beyond that, but I'd like to.'

'Me, too,' he said softly. Unexpectedly. He had never thought he would be in this situation, so any answer he gave would have been unexpected. But wanting this child? He needed a moment to process because he did. He wanted this child.

'Look, I know things are...weird between us, but this child is going to need us. Both of us. We need to give them the best that we can, and we'll need to work together.' She moved away from him, clutching her handbag closer to herself. 'I can put my feelings aside so our child can have the kind of parents and family we didn't.'

He should have thought about that. About being a parent, about his parents, about himself. He didn't want his child to have the same life he had. He wanted better for them.

'You're right.'

'I know.' Her lips curved into a small smile. 'Why don't we take the day to…process? We can meet tomorrow morning to talk about things.'

He nodded again.

'I'll send you a message with the details,' she said. Then she was gone. As if she'd never been there at all.

But she had been there. Today, and almost seven weeks ago now when she'd come with him to Italy. She'd changed his life. She'd shown him what it was like when someone cared about him. She'd helped him grow. She'd offered him love and understood even when he couldn't offer it to her in return. At least not in the way she needed it. Now, she was giving him a family.

With one glance at the door, he opened the file with the video of his baby. Watched it for a long time. Knew he'd hear the sound of the child's heart beating in his dreams that night. And the next. Maybe for ever. It wouldn't be such a bad thing.

The longer he listened to it, the more grounded he felt. The more courageous he felt. This child gave him hope. He'd have an opportunity to do things the way they were supposed to be done. He would give his child the things he didn't have. Love, support, a family. His child would give him the same, if he allowed it.

Elena would have given him the same, if he'd allowed it.

He sat back, the truth of it hitting him over the head. Of course, he already knew on some level that he was in love with her. Why else would he be so terrified of letting her in? He compared her to his parents even though she didn't deserve it. He compared her to his parents even though, in Italy, he'd already known she wasn't like them. She'd offered herself to him unconditionally, and he'd been too cowardly to accept. Or to offer himself to her in return.

It didn't mean that he didn't feel the same way about her. He loved her, but telling her would mean risking rejection. He was tired of rejection. He was tired of working so hard not to face it, but having to face it anyway. It was a fine thing to worry about after he'd rejected his own parents. After he'd rejected her.

Now they were having a kid, and he felt so stupid it had taken that for him to be brave. But that little heartbeat asked him to be brave. Even if it was too late, he needed to try. If there was a chance his child wouldn't have to witness a broken relationship as he'd had to with his parents, he had to take it. If there was a chance he could be with the woman he loved enough to have a family with, he had to try. Elena had every right to reject him now, but he wouldn't let that stop him. This was the final step to freeing himself from his past with his parents. And freeing himself would mean fullness. Happiness. Love.

He'd known about Elena's pregnancy for all of thirty minutes, but it had already changed him. And *that* was what love from a parent to a child should look like. Courage. Growth. Trying. His child would never know what conditional love would feel like. There would be no hoops for them to jump through; there would only be love.

He hoped he had the opportunity to treat Elena the same way.

CHAPTER NINETEEN

ELENA KNEW HAVING a child was a life-changing experience. She hadn't expected finding out she was pregnant would be as dramatic.

After leaving Micah's office the day before, she'd gone home and cried. Not because she was pregnant—though heaven knew there was some of that in there, too—but because she missed him. She wanted him back in her life. She wanted them to raise their baby together and be a family.

It took her a while to realise she would have all of those things now that she was having their baby. Not in the package she wanted, but she would have them, nevertheless. For it to work, she would need to set her feelings aside. Her desire to not be around Micah so he didn't remind her of what she didn't have no longer mattered. Her biggest responsibility now was her child. And since she'd told Micah it was possible for her to ignore her feelings, she wiped up her tears and faced her reality.

Still, she didn't sleep much that night, her mind too busy processing. The one good thing was that it helped her realise her child deserved the love Elena didn't have in her life. All things considered, it would be nice to explore that with a child. Special, too, because she'd made that child with someone she cared about. It wasn't a perfect situation, but that was okay. She would focus on her baby and let that heal her.

The doorbell rang promptly at eight the next morning. She expected nothing less from the man she'd married.

'Hey,' she said when she opened the door. 'I thought it would be easier to meet here. More private, too. There's been some interest in our relationship since the article.'

'I heard,' Micah said. 'Can I come in? This is heavy.'

She nodded, letting him pass. He was carrying a box, which he set on her kitchen counter. It was strange seeing him in her space. It obviously wasn't the first time he'd been there, but she hadn't been paying attention then.

But seeing him between her brown couches and cream walls and her various gold accents caused something in her chest to swell.

'You heard? I'm sorry,' she said with a wince. 'You've probably been teased about it.'

'No.' His expression told her that was the most ridiculous thing he'd heard. She resisted her smile. 'My father told me.'

'Your father?'

'He seemed to think marriage solicited a dinner invitation.'

She waited a beat. 'Your tone tells me little else solicited dinner invitations.'

'Nothing else,' he corrected.

'Well. I guess it's good that he's trying.' Again, his expression told her it wasn't good. 'How did the dinner go?'

'I didn't accept.'

'Why not?'

He shrugged. 'I'm done jumping through hoops for people who should love me unconditionally.'

'Oh. Wow.'

They stared at one another for a few seconds, then both started laughing softly.

'It's a good realisation,' she offered.

'It could have come a bit earlier,' he replied with a small smile.

'We all learn things at our own pace.'

'Yeah, we do.'

The amusement faded, but their eye contact remained. They were communicating on some level. Since she didn't know what level that was, and he wasn't offering anything more, she gestured to the box.

'What, er…what's in the box?'

He turned and looked at the box as if he hadn't brought it. She went to his side while she waited for an answer.

'It's for you,' he said after a long pause.

'It is?' She frowned when he pushed it towards her slightly. 'What's inside?'

'A care package.'

'A…'

She stopped speaking when she opened the box and saw what he meant. The box was filled to the brim with items. Herbal teas, crackers, ginger biscuits, books about pregnancy, movies about pregnancy, chocolate, chips, cocoa butter and stretch mark cream, a framed photo of their baby that he must have got from the video she'd shown him the day before. There was much more, but her hands faltered as she felt a strange tightness in her throat.

'You put this together?'

He ran a hand over his head. 'I looked up things that would be helpful to you. I didn't know about the creams and stuff, but a woman at the nature store helped me. She also said a cup of peppermint or chamomile tea would help with stress. That could help with your appetite thing.'

'I thought I said that wasn't a part of my pregnancy.'

'It can't make it any easier, can it?'

'No. It can't.'

She sat down on the kitchen stool in front of her counter and rested her hands in her head. The tightness in her throat had progressed to a burning at her eyes. She didn't think she'd cry, but she was pretty close to it. She spied a glass bottle of lemonade in the box—lemonade? Why?—and she reached in and took a sip. The sourness distracted her from the way her body was reacting. It helped her get her emotions under control.

Or not.

'You can't keep doing this.'

'What?'

'Reminding me that you're a great guy.'

'Oh.'

He looked as if he wanted to say more, but he didn't. So she said, 'I'm sorry. I shouldn't have said that. We should talk about the baby, right? Okay. I think—'

'Elena.'

'No, Micah. I can't... We can't do this.'

'Elena.'

She felt the tears falling down her cheeks. 'I'm sorry. I just... I need more time. I'll be okay with how things are between us soon. I promise. So let's just—'

'Damn it, Elena, look at me.' His voice was edged with desperation. It was reflected in his eyes when she met his gaze. 'I was a fool for pushing you away. That has nothing to do with the baby, and everything to do with me.' He hissed out a breath. 'I guess what I'm trying to say is that I love you. I love you, and I want to try again.'

In his dream the night before, Elena had fallen into his arms and told him she wanted to try again, too. But he was wide awake now. He knew that because now she was simply sitting, staring at him. He deserved it, he told himself, his heart thudding. He deserved the torture of waiting for her to say something.

'I think I misheard you,' she said slowly.

'You didn't.'

He reached over and took her hand. Prayed she wouldn't pull away. Then got distracted by the way she felt. Even in his dreams, he hadn't been able to capture what it was like when Elena touched him. The heat, the need, but, most importantly, the rightness that settled inside him.

'You're right, I pushed you away. I was scared. Scared you would be like my parents and reject me.' His grip tightened on her hand. Still, she didn't pull away. 'I don't know what it's like to love someone and have them love me back. I *do* know what it's like to love someone, and have them not love me the way I need to be loved.'

'Yeah, it sucks,' she said sullenly.

His lips curved. 'I know. And I'm sorry I made you feel that way because I didn't want to trust that first part. The part where I love you and you love me back.'

'You hurt me,' she said in a small voice. 'In the same way my parents hurt me. In the same way your parents hurt you.'

'I know. I know,' he said for the third time in as many minutes. 'I'm so sorry, Elena. If you'll let me, I'll spend the rest of my life making it up to you.'

She didn't speak for a long time. At first, he struggled against his instincts. He wanted to pull her into his arms, tell her they could be a family, kiss her, then take her to her bedroom and make love to her. But none of what he wanted mattered. It was only her, and her choice, and whatever that was, he would respect it.

But she was still holding his hand. That had to mean something.

'Do you really love me?' she asked. 'Not the baby—*me*. Would you have come here and told me this if it wasn't for the baby?

He took a breath. 'Yes. But probably not for a long time.' At her frown, he explained. 'I was already on my way to realising how stupid I'd been. I didn't only speak with my father, but my mother, too—later—' he said when she opened her mouth '—and I realised that they weren't worth the effort I was putting into them. They'd taught me to fear love, but they weren't worth what I was sacrificing with you.'

He pushed her hair back.

'But realising it didn't mean I had the courage to come here and tell you that. I would have needed time to, and maybe a knock over the head. Or a pregnancy surprise.' He gave her a small smile. 'But I would have told you regardless, I promise. Because I love you, and I have, probably since I saw you in that unicorn nightshirt and you told me I didn't see them because I didn't believe.'

'I'm not sure that's what I said.'

'We can argue about it later,' he teased, but sobered quickly. 'If you still want me here later.'

'I'll always want you here,' she said softly. 'My love for you isn't conditional. Even when you're being dumb, I still love you.'

'You know exactly what to say, don't you?' he asked, but before he was even done talking, she was hugging him so tightly he could barely breathe.

'I'm scared, too, you know. But I love you. I love you.'

His arms folded around her. 'I know you're scared. But you're braver than me. You're stronger than me. Our baby is going to have a wonderful mother.' He lifted her chin. 'You don't have to be scared any more. Your love is safe with me. Believe me.'

Her lips curved. 'I do. And yours is safe with me. You're safe with me.'

Her expression told him she would make sure he knew it for the rest of their lives.

And he would do the same for her. That understanding, their love, meant more to him than he could express. So he leaned forward and kissed her instead.

EPILOGUE

Four years later

'WHO THOUGHT BRINGING two children to Italy was a good idea?'

'I believe that was you,' Elena said easily, lifting her son's ice-cream cone when he tilted it to the side to lick his fingers. 'You said something about bringing them to where our love was established, or something equally corny.'

'You used to think that was charming.'

'Now I think you carrying a baby girl in a carrier at the front of your body is charming.' She brushed the hand she didn't hold her son with over the head of the baby gurgling against Micah's chest. 'It's also very sexy.'

She leaned forward and kissed him, lingering even though she probably shouldn't have.

'Hmm,' Micah murmured when she pulled away. 'How long until naptime?'

As if answering, Kai shouted, 'Bird!' at her feet. It startled his sister, and Ellie immediately gave a loud cry.

Elena laughed. 'Two children in Italy is not as romantic as two adults in Italy.'

'That's for sure,' Micah said, comforting Ellie.

Elena followed Kai to the pigeons, warning him against feeding them his ice cream. She'd learnt that lesson the hard way her first time in Italy.

She'd learnt a lot since her first time in Italy. To be fair, it had been almost four years ago. She'd got married and had two children since then. Her job was still important to her, though a little less than her family was, and her recent promotion seemed to prove it. The newspaper was undeterred by her family planning, which she knew made her lucky. She also knew she had a unique angle on many of the stories their readers were interested in. The wife of a South African businessperson who wasn't afraid of telling the truth.

Fortunately, she had a husband who supported her.

They'd taken their time to build the foundation of their marriage. It was a strange approach considering they were married within a week of knowing one another and pregnant after their wedding night. But they'd both been hurt by their families. They'd made progress, even before they'd decided to try a relationship, but it still took work. And they put in the work. In between pregnancy and caring for an infant. In between caring for a toddler and finding out they were pregnant again.

Relationships took constant work, and neither of them was afraid of it. In fact, they welcomed it. Because working meant they still wanted to be there. They still wanted one another. It was a damn good feeling to be wanted.

'I don't suppose we could take them on a gondola ride,' Elena remarked later that day. 'No—what am I saying? Kai would be in the water within minutes.'

Micah laughed. They'd swapped children, both of whom were asleep, exhausted by the excitement of the day. She and Micah were walking back to the hotel, but lazily, the summer's day not dictating haste.

'Last time I was in a gondola I spontaneously proposed. Perhaps this family is not made for gondola rides.'

Now Elena laughed. 'Ah, we were such babies then. Could you imagine being where we are now, then? You, dominating the luxury goods industry. Me, dominating childbirth.' She shook her head. 'What powerful parents we are.'

'One more powerful than the other.' Micah made sure Kai was secure, then put an arm around Elena. 'I watched you give birth. It was...wild.'

'A euphemistic way to put that.' She leaned into him. 'I think this is the happiest I've ever been.'

'You say that all the time.'

'I mean it every time. More so today.' She stopped walking and turned to him. 'Our first family trip is to Italy. I wasn't this lucky. You weren't either. But we're doing it for our kids. There's a lot to be grateful for.'

'They won't remember this, you know,' Micah said, but his expression was soft. 'It didn't matter where we took them on vacation.'

'That's obviously not my point.'

'I know.' He lowered and kissed her gently. 'You're what these kids will be most grateful for some day. I know that because that's how I feel.'

'Right back at you, Daddy.'

'I thought we agreed you wouldn't ever call me that in public.'

'I thought you would keep a sentimental moment sacred, but you didn't. You used logic. So I guess we'll both just be disappointed then, won't we?'

Micah laughed and they resumed walking. It was companionable and quiet. It was perfect.

'Remind me to ask Kai about the pigeons when he wakes up,' Micah said suddenly.

'What about the pigeons?'

'I want to know if he thinks the ones in Europe are different from those in Africa, like his mother.'

She slapped him lightly on the shoulder, and his laughter echoed in the dusk.

* * * * *